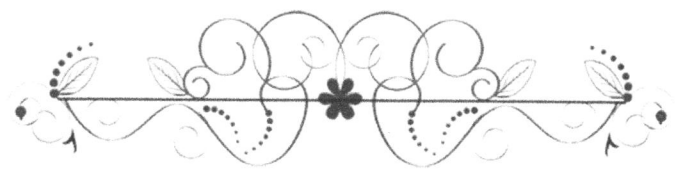

To Mr. Storm. I did, I do, and I always will.

A FREE GIFT FOR YOU!

Thank you for picking up your copy of *Love's Vow*. I so hope you love it! As a thank-you, I'd like to offer you a free gift. That's right, I've written a short story that's available exclusively to my newsletter subscribers. You'll receive the free story by e-mail as soon as you sign up at www.MelStorm.com/Gift. I hope you'll enjoy both stories. Happy reading!

ONE

Summer Smith laced up her running shoes and headed outside. This was her last Tuesday as a single woman. Soon she would join the Davis family as Ben's wife. She could still scarcely believe that the tiny Texas town of Sweet Grove had become the setting of her real-life happily ever after.

She'd only meant to stay for the summer, both to help her aunt Iris run the small flower shop in town and to figure out what she wanted most from life. As a little girl, she'd pictured herself jet-setting all over the world in search of her next great adventure. Funny how the greatest adventure of all had been falling in love—not just with Ben, but with the town, its people, and with the God she now understood worked miracles.

She jogged past Ernie's on her way to the old orchard that lay to the north of town. The little German restaurant had been the scene of her first date with Ben—a date that had been so uncomfortably formal she never could have guessed they'd one day end up here, on their way to the altar, their way to forever.

Turning into the park, Summer felt as if she could run for days without stopping. When her fiancé had first invited her to hit the trails with him, she'd laughed off his suggestion. But when he asked a second time and then a third, she decided she might as well give it a shot. Summer had always kept a healthy diet, but she'd never been the type to exercise for fun. Not until she found a new kind of exhilaration in racing Ben through town in the mornings and watching as all of Sweet Grove woke up to begin a new day.

Soon she and Ben would wake up for each day together, a thought that both thrilled and terrified her. She was going to be somebody's wife! And not just *any*body, but the somebody she loved most in the entire world. Ben often liked to claim that she had saved his life, but he failed to see that he had saved hers right back. After all, a life without purpose wasn't much of a life at all.

Now she had her dream job as the editor for the

Sweet Grove Sentinel, a close-knit group of friends who still met every Thursday night for karaoke, and a home that suited her perfectly. And her groom-to-be had also discovered how much he already had to be thankful for. He said it was because her mixed-up flower delivery had stopped him from taking his own life, but now they both knew that it was God who had saved Ben that day.

"Ben!" she called, spotting him standing on the bridge farther down the path.

"There's my bride!"

"A bride in running shoes and spandex? Sure." Summer giggled and returned Ben's kisses.

"Why not? Maybe I don't want to wait. Maybe I want to marry you right here, right now." He nipped at her lip playfully before pulling back and smiling down at her.

"Just a few more days to go." She laced her fingers through Ben's and stood with him at the edge of the bridge looking out over the creek. Two of her favorite memories had happened right here where they stood now. First they'd made their promises to themselves that they would no longer be afraid of life, and then a few months later, they'd made a promise to each other when Ben had asked her to marry him in front of the entire town.

As she watched the soft ripples move below, she

couldn't picture being any happier than she was now in this moment, in *all the moments* with Ben.

Ben traced kisses across her neck and mumbled, "What am I going to do without you?"

"It's only for a few days."

"I can barely get through an afternoon without seeing you, and now you're asking me to spend four whole days without you?" A wicked grin crossed his face, and he said, "What if I refuse?"

She turned away when he tried to kiss her. "C'mon, Ben. It's hard for me, too. But you know it will make our big day even more special."

"I'm marrying my dream girl," he said. "Nothing could be more special than that."

She was about to argue, but he raised a finger to her lips and said, "But I'll do whatever I have to do to make my bride happy."

"You've been talking with Pastor Bernie," she said with a laugh.

"Happy wife, happy life," he mimicked in a spot-on impression of the First Street Church minister.

The thing was, Summer already felt happier than she ever thought she could be. If this was the way the rest of her life would play out, too . . . well, that would just be heaven on earth.

* * *

Ben scooped Summer into his arms and carried her away from the bridge.

"What are you doing?" She wrapped her arms around his neck and stared at him lovingly as he brought her over to the picnic breakfast he had set up deeper into the orchard.

"Practicing carrying you over the threshold," he said matter-of-factly.

"Well, good job." She laughed and gave him a quick peck before hopping from his arms and back to a standing position of her own.

"It's not quite breakfast in bed, but, hey, what can you do?" Ben said as they both settled onto the sheet he'd spread out under a nearby tree that was full of beautiful pink blooms.

"Does this mean breakfast in bed is something I can look forward to in the future?" she asked, opening the drawstring bag Ben had packed and pulling out a pair of apple turnovers he'd purchased from Jack Bryant's mill on the way in.

"Yup, you'll be living the high life once you're Mrs. Davis," he answered with a wink.

"Mmm, I like the sound of that." She took a big bite of the pastry and let out a moan. "And the taste of this. Mmm."

"Stop making me crazy, please. It's been hard

enough waiting nearly a year to make you mine. You making all those cute noises does not help."

"Mmm, mmm," Summer said with a laugh. "So yummy!"

"Okay, that's it!" He took her turnover away and placed it on a napkin, then pushed her down onto the sheet and covered her face and neck with kisses.

"Mr. Davis, I'm scandalized!" she cried, bringing a hand to her chest and making a ridiculous face. That was Summer, though. Any excuse to show off her "actressing" skills.

He held his weight on each of his arms as he stared down at Summer, whose brown hair lay fanned out in soft waves The blonde highlights mixed throughout caught the sun and shone like gold. "I'd wait an eternity for you, but that doesn't mean I'd like it."

Summer held up her hands and wiggled her fingers playfully. "Four more days, but if you're going to misbehave I suppose we could put off the wedding until next year."

Ben scrambled back, putting a good foot of distance between himself and his fiancée. "I'm the perfect gentleman, see!" he insisted.

She laughed and shook her head. "Yes, you are. Now give me my apple thingy back, please."

"Fine, you win."

"Happy wife, happy life," they both said at the same time and then broke apart in laughter again. Summer scooted over on the sheet until their hips were touching and then gave Ben a kiss on his cheek.

"I love you," she said.

"I loved you first."

"Oh, so now it's a competition?"

"Maybe."

"If you really want a competition, then race me to the well."

He eyed her with a half-cocked grin. "What do I get if I win?"

"To marry me," she answered pertly, shoving the rest of the pastry into her mouth and then licking her fingers.

"And if I lose?"

"To marry me," she said again. That was his Summer, the eternal optimist. She showed him that life didn't have to be all black or white. It could be rose-colored, too.

He grinned at her, knowing he'd easily win the race but that he'd probably let her win, anyway. "Okay, then you're on."

Ben stood and began to pack up their picnic, but before he could finish, Summer took off like a shot.

"No fair!" he cried, running after her.

"Fair is for losers," she called as he picked up speed and passed her.

"What was that?" he yelled over his shoulder. "I couldn't hear you from so far away."

He kept his pace steady so that he finished just narrowly ahead of Summer. He loved how much she was getting into jogging these past few months, but he still had years of conditioning on her.

"I win," he pointed out as he dropped his bag on the hill and stood with Summer in front of the old wishing well.

"Okay, fine, so you get to marry me."

"Awesome," he said.

"Awesome," she said, reaching into her sock and pulling out a shiny pair of pennies.

"What's this for?" he asked.

She looked from him to the well and back again. "Umm, do I really have to explain what to do at a wishing"—she forced an exaggerated series of coughs—"well?"

"Ha ha, very funny. But did it ever occur to you that maybe I already have everything I ever wished for?"

If her face wasn't already red from the run, Ben was sure his words would have brought fresh color to her cheeks. "Just make a wish, Ben," she said, hitting him playfully.

"How about you make two?" he suggested.

She raised both pennies and studied them in the sunlight. "Hmm, I had one, but I don't think I can think of a second."

"See?" He gloated. "When life gives you lemonade, it's hard to think of the lemons."

"I don't think that's how the saying goes."

"Will you feel better if I make a wish?" he asked with a laugh.

"Yes, please."

"Okay, then." He took one of the pennies from her, still unable to think of a wish he'd like to make for himself. So, instead, he wished that his mother might find happiness like this again one day for herself.

"Ready?" Summer asked.

He nodded, and together they both tossed their wishes down into the old well. He prayed his would come true sooner rather than later, feeling a moment of sadness when he thought of his mother's suffering over the years.

But then Summer was running back toward the orchard, laughing and teasing him—and it was hard to remember that there had ever been any sadness in his life. Or to imagine that there'd ever be any again.

TWO

Summer floated home on cloud nine. It felt so cliché, but she really *did* love Ben more with each passing day. Imagine how enamored she'd be fifty years from now!

Her smile disappeared the moment she stepped into the house and found her aunt's conure, Sunny Sunshine, screeching at the top of his little bird lungs as Aunt Iris clopped around the house wearing rubber boots and waving about a hand rake.

"You are not helping, Sunny boy!" her aunt said, frowning at the parrot.

"What's going on here?" Summer demanded, charging into the room and relieving her klutzy aunt of the sharp tool before she could hurt herself.

"Oh, Summer, I'm so sorry! It's all ruined!"

"What's ruined?"

Aunt Iris turned and waved for Summer to follow her outside into the garden. Everything looked fine to Summer's untrained eye, but then again, she was terrible when it came to flowers—the very fact that led her to find Ben in the first place.

"I can't look!" Iris shrieked, dramatically shielding her eyes. "It's just too terrible!"

Summer shifted her weight from one foot to the other as Iris dropped to her knees and began digging in the garden bed with another hand tool. "Umm, everything looks fine to me," Summer said at last. "What exactly is the matter?"

Iris sighed and wiped a bead of sweat from her brow, leaving behind an ugly brown smudge as she did. "All I wanted was to grow a beautiful garden for your wedding. It was my gift to you and Ben, so that one day when I'm gone and leave the house to you, you can wake up every morning and look out the window to remember your special day and the aunt who loved you so much." Her normally cheery aunt was as close to tears as Summer had ever seen her, and it broke Summer's heart.

She bent down and slung a comforting arm over her aunt's shoulder. "Stop that, you. You have at least another fifty good years in you."

"Because living to be one hundred and ten runs in the family?" Iris sniffed, then let out a chuckle.

"Well, you always were a trendsetter." Summer jabbed her aunt playfully before trying to broach the subject of the mysterious problem again. "So can you tell me what's going on?"

Iris leaned forward and cupped a green bud in her hand. "See this? This is your bed of asters. I know they're your favorite, so I planted extras so that the full altar could be woven with asters."

Summer gasped. "Oh, Aunt Iris. That sounds beautiful."

"Well, don't get too attached to the idea, because they are late blooming this year, and judging by the look of this bud, they won't be blooming until *after* the big day."

"Okay, so we won't have asters. Can we use daisies? You know I can't tell the difference anyway." She laughed, but her aunt's mood didn't lighten. Iris didn't even take the time to explain that daisies were a type of aster, as she normally would.

"If that were the only problem we were facing, sure. But there's more." Aunt Iris crossed the yard and stopped in front of a patch of oleanders.

"See this little guy here? He's an aphid, and I can guarantee you he's brought more than a thousand of his closest friends to vacation in the garden."

"So we'll call the exterminator," Summer suggested.

"Yes, and kill all the flowers in the process," Iris moaned.

"What happens if you just leave them alone?"

"They'll chew the edges of the petals and swarm your guests."

"Okay, so maybe there's not really an upside to that." Summer bit down on her lower lip as she thought. "I love that you wanted to do this for us, Aunt Iris, but it's okay, really. I just want to marry Ben. I can do that anywhere, and you're going to live for a long, long while yet, so you have many more years to work on making the garden perfect."

"But what kind of florist does that make me? I'm failing my flowers when it matters most." If Aunt Iris had been the crying type, tears would have surely fallen then, watering the derelict garden all around them.

"Aunt Iris, stop that. You don't control the weather or the whims of icky little bugs. Besides, now Ben and I can get married inside the church. That will be nice, won't it?"

"But—"

"Keep working on the garden. I know we'll have a use for it someday. Maybe we can renew our vows here or christen our first child, or—hey—maybe you can get married under an arch of asters?"

"Oh, dear Summer," Aunt Iris said with a smile at last. "You know my favorite flower is the tulip."

When Ben's phone buzzed in his pocket, he knew it must be Summer. He glanced down at the tiny screen, and—sure enough—it was his fiancée calling with a wedding emergency.

"Ben, change of plans," she said, skipping straight past hello. "Aunt Iris's house is out of commission. We need to have the rehearsal dinner—and the wedding—somewhere else."

"Do I even want to know what happened?" he asked, then listened as Summer talked about bugs and asters and inheritances, all the while wringing his brain for the simplest solution.

"What if we got married at the church?" he asked.

"That's what I was thinking, too. Do you mind giving Pastor Bernie a call?"

"I'm on it. You go calm your aunt down."

"Believe me, I'm trying," she answered with a sigh that suggested he got the easy end of the deal here. "Will you let the others know about the change, too?"

"I'll take care of everything," he promised. "I love you, and I'll see you tonight."

He hung up with Summer and said a quick prayer that everything would turn out all right. Thankfully, they lived in a small town where last-minute changeups like this were possible.

The pastor answered on the first ring. "Ahh, Ben. Ready for tonight?" Why did nobody ever answer with a hello?

He paced the length of his room as he spoke. "I am, but our venue is not. Would it be okay for us to have the wedding and rehearsal at the church? I know it's last minute, but there are some unexpected problems at Iris's."

"Oh, dear. Well, we can have the wedding at the church, but I'm afraid it's unavailable tonight. You see, we've had ourselves a termite scare, and there are parts of the floor missing right now. It'll be fixed by Sunday, but as for tonight. Well, it just won't work."

Ben cursed under his breath.

"What was that, Ben?" Pastor Bernie asked, and Ben could just picture the pastor's red eyebrows raised in shock at Ben's colorful choice of language.

"Sorry," he whispered into the phone. "I just want everything to be perfect."

"It will be," Bernie said. A muffled exchange followed, and Ben waited for the pastor to return with a sudden solution. Perhaps the church could be made available, after all.

He returned a short bit later, his voice now crisp and clear as he announced, "Tabitha wants to talk to you."

"Hello, Ben," the pastor's wife said sweetly as she took over the Olsons' end of the conversation. "Can you have the rehearsal at Mabel's? You'll be headed there anyway for dinner, right? The rehearsal for the ceremony will only take about half an hour. You might as well combine venues for the night."

"Hey, that's a great idea. I'll give Jeffrey a call now to check."

"Oh, I'm so glad to hear it." He could almost hear Tabitha's grin through the phone line. She was such a kind woman, though he barely had cause to interact with her. Tabitha oversaw many of the women's activities with the church and volunteered around town, but Ben only really saw her when she came to the market for her weekly grocery trip.

"Thank you," he said with a huge sigh of relief. "And please thank the pastor for me, too."

"Of course. Buh-bye now," she said, ending their call.

After another hour of placing phone calls to the various members of their wedding party, it was all decided. The rehearsal would take place at Mabel's, the wedding at the church, and everything else would go off without a hitch.

Four more days and Summer would be his forever. Four more hours and they'd be ready to practice the ceremony that would bring them together once and for all. Until then, he had some time to kill, which meant he could work on his vows until they felt perfect.

When Summer had suggested they write their own vows, Ben had been quick to agree. Shortly after, though, he realized he was way out of his element. Summer was the writer, not him. He'd worked and reworked his vows dozens of times now, but they still didn't feel right.

"Dear sweet Summer," he read aloud as he flipped through his notecards and reviewed the latest version of said vows. "Webster defines marriage as . . . Ugh, this is awful," he said to himself, crumbling up the notecard and tossing it into the wastebasket. He took out the next card and read, "In Roman times, couples would literally tie the knot by . . ."

Hmm, maybe he needed to sleep on it. Then again, there were only four sleeps left until the big day. Would it be enough to find the words that would convey what he felt in his heart?

THREE

Summer couldn't think of a better place than Mabel's on Maple to hold their wedding rehearsal. True, Aunt Iris's garden would have been lovely, too, but the old-fashioned diner on Main Street was the heart and soul of Sweet Grove every bit as much as the little white church on First Street.

When she arrived that evening, she found the tables and chairs had already been pushed aside to create an aisle, and the big window in back was decorated with folded napkins and colorful streamers to create a makeshift altar.

"I love it," she said, letting a slow breath out as she finished. This town and its people never ceased to amaze her with their generosity and creativity.

"Well, you'd better!" Mabel said with a sly smile.

"We're closing down shop for the rest of the night just for you."

"Oh, I didn't mean to cost you business, Mabel. Wait a sec. Aren't you retired?"

"Technically, but this diner still has my name on it, you know. And you aren't costing us anything, Sum. The whole town will be here tonight to celebrate you and Ben. Business is booming." Mabel waggled her eyebrows before racing back toward the kitchen.

As soon as Mabel had disappeared, Summer's maid of honor, Elise, came into the diner balancing a giant cardboard box of wedding favors in her outstretched arms. Summer had had an impossible time picking which of her new friends should fill the role, but luckily Elise decided for her, stating she would do the honors before Summer had the chance to ask her or anyone else.

"Oh, let me help you with that!" Mabel reappeared in a while and tried to grab the box from Elise.

"I don't think so!" Kristina Rose shouted from the little food window that divided the kitchen and the dining room. "Do you want to have another heart attack?"

"I survived the first one, didn't I?" Mabel asked with a chuckle.

"Okay, that's it." Kristina Rose stomped into the

main dining area and took her former boss by the hand, pulling her toward a side booth.

"I'm not a child," Mabel argued.

"You sure are acting like one. You may not care about your health, but I do. Now sit."

Summer looked to Elise, who shrugged.

"She's got a point," her friend whispered.

"If you want to help, there's plenty you can do from a *seated* position," Kristina Rose offered. "For starters, we still have many more napkins to fold into flowers."

"Fine," Mabel griped as she rolled her eyes at Kristina Rose.

During the hustle and bustle of the restauranteurs' argument, Iris breezed into the diner next followed by Jennifer, Liam, and Molly Sue. Ben still hadn't turned up, and it wasn't like him to be late.

"How's my beautiful flower girl?" Summer asked, giving Molly Sue a tight hug.

Molly Sue coughed without covering her mouth, spraying Summer with a stream of spittle right in her face.

"Sorry," the little girl sniffed. "Daddy, can I help fold napkins?" she asked, turning toward Liam and running her hand across her nose.

"I don't think that's such a good idea. You may be contagious."

"Jennifer, can I?" she said, turning to her new stepmother. Liam and Jennifer had eloped only a few weeks before and were still finding their way as a married couple.

"Sure. Just wash your hands really good first, okay?" she said, then turned to a frowning Liam as their daughter skipped away toward the bathroom.

"It's okay," Summer insisted. "It's so sweet she wants to help. It's probably just allergies this time of year anyway. It'll be fine."

Just then, a blurb of orange zoomed overhead, landing on the chandelier overhead. Summer wasn't in the least bit startled. She'd grown used to Sunny Sunshine's antics after living almost a full year with the little parrot.

Aunt Iris pulled a chair to the center of the checkered floor and climbed on top of it. "C'mon, Sunny boy. It's safe here. You don't have to be scared." She spoke softly to her pet, but he still refused to budge, sidestepping away from her as she tried to retrieve him from the light fixture.

"This looks like a job for somebody with a few extra inches on his frame," Pastor Bernie said, having arrived during the chaos. "Besides we gingers have to stick together. Right, Sunny Sunshine?"

Sunny Sunshine chirruped angrily and fluffed the feathers on his neck.

Iris stepped down from the chair and allowed Bernie to climb up.

"C'mon, little guy," Bernie said as he lifted an index finger toward the bird's chest to allow him to step up.

"Ouch, you little devil!" he cried a second later, recoiling as the little parrot clamped down onto his outstretched finger.

"My Sunny is not a devil!" Iris spat. "He's just scared is all."

The pastor sucked on his wounded finger. "Sorry. It was just a reaction from the pain. I didn't mean to say that, but I'm also not too eager to try again with Sunny. So much for the ginger brotherhood."

"We could sing to him to help calm him down," Summer's aunt suggested. "You are my sunshine," she started.

At which point, Ben arrived with his mother, Susan, who joined in the refrain with her well-practiced soprano. She'd recently rejoined the church choir and had fallen in love with music all over again as a result.

"There's a good bird," Iris cooed, scooping the bird off the chandelier and cuddling him to her chest. "I'm sorry we startled you. Probably best to go back in the cage until your part in the wedding comes up."

Once Iris had scuttled away, Pastor Bernie whispered to Ben and Summer, "Are you sure it's such a good idea to have that bird as ring bearer? He nearly took my finger off!" He held out his hand to show the angry red beak indent just above his knuckle.

"Ow, sorry about that," Ben said, placing an arm over Summer's shoulders and pulling her into his side. "I think Sunny's already a lock, though. Summer?"

Summer frowned. "Aunt Iris is already so upset about the garden. If we kick Sunny out of the wedding, too, she will be devastated. I'm sorry, Pastor Bernie. But maybe we can come up with a plan so you don't have to touch him again."

"No worries, I understand," the pastor said with a chuckle. "I'll just go help Jeffrey with the final details for tonight."

"What a circus," Ben said with a laugh, then gave Summer a kiss on her cheek.

"None of this upsets you?" she asked her fiancé.

"It's actually kind of perfect," he answered. "It reminds me of the time Sunny escaped outside and everyone turned up to help. It's like all of our relationship's greatest hits in one big, beautiful disaster of a rehearsal dinner."

"Well, I'm glad you find it amusing," she said with a sigh. "I just want everyone to be happy, especially Aunt Iris."

"I just want to be married to you," her perfect groom answered.

"Okay, are we ready to say our practice I do's?" the pastor asked, returning to the dining room with Jeffrey, who was also Ben's best man, at his heels.

"Is everybody here?" Summer asked, looking around at the sea of smiling faces that crowded the dining room. They'd only invited their closest friends and relatives to the rehearsal dinner, but that included at least half the town of Sweet Grove.

"Umm, almost," Susan spoke up, her voice quavering as she did.

"Who are we waiting on, Mom?" Ben asked. Summer hoped that one day she would be comfortable calling her mother-in-law *Mom*, too, but it just didn't feel natural yet.

"Your father," she said to Ben.

And with those two little words, her perfect groom lost his perfect smile for the night.

Ben's blood rushed to his head, and he had to sit down before he passed out.

Summer rubbed his back reassuringly, but not even she could make him feel better. This wedding was supposed to be for him and Summer, for all the people they both loved—it did not include his absentee father. The last thing he wanted was to start his new life by staring at the ugly wreckage of a life he had hated so much he'd thought of ending it with a bullet to the brain.

"He's your father," his mom argued. "He should be here."

"He stopped being my father a long time ago," Ben said through clenched teeth.

"Let's start the rehearsal now," Summer told the pastor. "No sense in delaying."

Ben held Summer's hands across the makeshift altar and nodded along as Bernie said his parts and had the couple repeat theirs. He should have been staring joyfully into his bride's eyes, reflecting on how much he loved her, and wondering what forever could hold for the two of them. Instead, though, his eyes kept darting nervously toward the door.

Any minute now his father would arrive and spoil everything. What an awesome reminder of how terribly wrong a marriage could go. And for some reason, his mother had helped to facilitate this. He'd really thought she was getting better since rehab, that she was reclaiming her life. So why would she invite his dad when neither of them wanted to see the man?

Summer squeezed his hands, bringing him back to the present. "Ben, I love you," she whispered so that only he and the pastor could hear. "No matter what," she promised.

The pastor smiled at them both. "Summer has asked that we save the vows until the big day so that they'll be a surprise, which means we'll skip that part in the recital. Moving forward, do we have the rings?" Pastor Bernie asked.

"Coming!" Aunt Iris called, marching forward with Sunny Sunshine perched on a pink satin pillow.

"Ben, you'll go first." The pastor nodded to him and took a step back as Iris brought Sunny Sunshine and the pillow beside Ben.

He would have laughed if he weren't so preoccupied with the worry over his father. Instead, he just wanted to get this night over with. Maybe they could finish before his father had a chance to show, or maybe he wouldn't even show at all. Ben grabbed for the ring, and the sun conure grabbed for his finger—and bit down hard.

He tried to pull his hand back, but the bird would not let go.

"Sunny, no!" Iris cried.

"Ouch, ouch, ouch!" Ben cried.

"*Squawk!*" Sunny Sunshine cried, finally letting go of Ben's poor, throbbing finger.

"Seems we have ourselves a club now. Welcome,

Ben." Pastor Bernie laughed, but Ben had too much pain both in his heart and on his finger to join in.

Bernie cleared his throat. "Umm, well, I think that's enough practice for tonight. Should we move on to dinner?"

Mabel popped up from her booth. "Yes, let's put the tables back and get to eating."

"Sit back down," Kristina Rose snapped. "Let those of us with good hearts handle the heavy lifting."

"Forget that little bite," Mabel mumbled to the pastor or maybe to Ben. "*That* hurt."

Everyone rushed to put the restaurant back in order, and in the frenzy, a few new guests arrived.

"What did we miss?" Ben's father, John Davis, asked, coming to stand behind his ex-wife.

There was that boiling feeling again. Ben hadn't seen his father in almost two years, but the man looked exactly as he remembered him—an aged version of Stephen, the brother who'd been taken from Ben far too soon. They both had the same sandy-brown hair, green eyes, square jaws. They were both tall and muscular, whereas Ben had more of a runner's build.

"Welcome to Sweet Grove. We're so glad you could make it." Susan politely extended a hand to her replacement, John's young news anchor wife, Megan, who held a curly-haired toddler straddled against her hip.

"No, we're not," Ben grumbled. "Why are you here anyway?" Ben shot daggers toward his father, wishing that his eyes could produce actual weapons to defend him and his mother from this intruder of the past.

"Because I love you, son, and I'm proud of you," John answered, opening his arms for a hug.

Ben crossed his arms over his chest. "Sure, whatever."

"Ben," Susan scolded. "Be nice to your father."

"He's not my father, at least he hasn't been for a long time."

"I'm sorry about his rude behavior," Susan said with a frown.

"Mom, do not apologize to him. If anything, he should apologize to us."

Ben felt all of his friends' eyes on him as they watched the heated exchange with his father. He didn't want to make a scene, didn't want to ruin this for Summer—but all reason left him when it came to the one man he hated more than any other in the whole world.

The toddler, Ben's little sister apparently, began to cry and ask for "piggy." Her mother rooted around in a huge diaper bag and pulled out a plush bear.

"Stephanie names all her toys *piggy*," she explained with a half laugh.

Ben hadn't thought he could hold any more anger in his heart, but hearing that name dropped so casually caused his heart to swell with rage.

"I'm sorry," his mother said. "What did you say her name was?"

"Stephanie," John answered. "We named her in Stephen's honor."

"Oh, I see," Susan said, turning her gaze to the floor. "Ben, if it's all right, I think I'll skip out on dinner. I'm not feeling very well all of a sudden."

"Mom, please, don't," Ben begged. He recognized the tremor in her hands, the hitch in her voice—and he refused to let her fall back into her old drinking patterns just because his imposter father had returned on a whim. "*He* can go instead."

"They only just got here. Let your father—"

"No, it's okay," John answered. "We'll come see you tomorrow, Ben. Susan." He nodded at each of them before placing his hand on the lower back of his far-too-young wife and directing her out of the restaurant.

"I wish you wouldn't," Ben called after him but wasn't sure whether he'd been heard.

Summer crept up beside him and laced her fingers between his. "It's going to be okay," she promised. "Soon we'll be on the beach far, far away."

"I love you," Ben said. "That's the only thing that matters."

"Yes, this day is for us, Ben. Don't let him get you down. At least he came. My dad's long gone, and my mom couldn't make the trip, but now you have both of your parents here. That's something to be thankful for, right?"

Ben shrugged. "I guess."

"It's only four more days," she pointed out.

Yes, only four more days, one hundred and thirteen hours, 6,780 minutes, 406,800 seconds . . . and Ben would be counting down every single one.

FOUR

Summer hated seeing Ben so hurt. With his father back in town, it was almost as if all the progress he'd made in coping with his depression was now wiped clean. She recognized the sullen expression and dull look in his eyes from when they'd first met almost a year ago. He'd been ready to take his own life then, and while depression wasn't an illness that could ever fully be cured, Ben had taken great strides toward living a happier life.

For her part, Summer had learned to read his body language, to figure whether he needed to be redirected toward something positive or given a bit of time to unwind and clear his brain. This time, though, neither of those techniques seemed to be the solution.

She smiled as much as she could and told him again and again how much she loved him during their rehearsal dinner, but his posture remained overly stiff and his face stayed stuck in a frown. This wasn't depression, but rather anger—which was almost the exact opposite.

Ben had always been a sensitive, kind man, and she had never seen him quite like this before. Maybe her idea to spend the rest of the week apart was a bad one, after all. Her fiancé needed her, and she needed to be there for him.

"Ben," she said, turning to him as they walked toward the door of Mabel's and prepared to go out into the night.

He grunted, which she took to mean he was listening.

"I don't want to—"

The moment they pushed the door open, a dark cloth covered Summer's face. She heard laughter and shrieks but couldn't see anything.

"Bye, I love you!" Ben shouted as Summer was forced into the front seat of a car.

"What's going on?" she demanded. "I need to get back to Ben. He—"

"Will be just fine," Elise answered from beside her, just seconds before the engine roared to life.

The familiar fragrance of strawberries drifted

forward from the back seat as Jennifer leaned forward and said, "We promise to be kind and benevolent captors," and then exploded in a giggle.

Kristina Rose spoke up next. "Guys, it's not really a surprise if we're all going to talk and give ourselves away. Maybe we should just take off her blindfold?"

"No!" Elise insisted. "This is the way they do it in the movies, so this is the way we're going to do it, too."

"Who cares about the movies?" Kristina Rose argued, but she seemed to be alone in her opinion.

"Oh, I wish that I could offer you a drink to calm your nerves," Maisie said, "but there's that pesky no-open-containers rule, and the last thing we need is a ticket. After all, it's *your* car."

"You kidnapped me *and* stole my car?" Summer squeaked. It was hot beneath the blindfold, and she longed to yank it off.

"As your maid of honor, it's up to me to make sure you end your single life in style," Elise pointed out. "Believe me, this will be a night to remember long after you become Mrs. Ben Davis."

"Speaking of *Mr.* Ben Davis," Summer said sadly, "I'm worried about him. Can I get a raincheck on whatever this is?"

"Why, I never," Elise gasped.

Jennifer leaned forward and spoke much too

loudly right next to Summer's ear. "No way! You only get one chance at a bachelorette party. Take it from someone who skipped out on hers. You don't want to miss this."

"Aww, Jenn," Maisie said. "I had no idea you felt that way. Maybe we can make tonight your party, too. Do you mind sharing, Summer?"

Summer shrugged. Sure, Jennifer could have this night all to herself. Summer had other things to worry about. She tried to answer, "I—"

"But I'm already married!" Jennifer argued.

"So what?" Elise crooned. "It's not like we're the kind of girls to hire a stripper and invite him back to our hotel room. This is just wild and crazy girl-bonding time, Sweet Grove style."

Kristina Rose spoke next. "I know you're worried about Ben, sweetie, but Pastor Bernie and the others will make sure he's taken care of. Susan, too. In fact, I'll call Jeffrey right now, if it will put your mind at ease."

They all waited as Kristina Rose placed a call to her boyfriend with the phone on speaker.

"Yes, of course. I have some bachelor party ideas of my own," Jeffrey said.

"Oooh, scandalous!" Jennifer said.

Jeffrey chuckled. "Nothing like that. We're having an all-night *Call of Duty* marathon."

"Sounds boring," Maisie said.

"Did you invite Liam?" Jennifer asked.

"Yeah, but he said no. It's not like we can't all play games after Ben gets married, so we'll get him another time."

"Okay, thanks, babe. I've gotta go."

"Bye. I love you," Kristina Rose said softly, and Summer could just picture the lovesick grin she most likely wore on her face as she said those three little words to her very own dream man.

"Love you, too," Jeffrey answered, then made a smacking noise in imitation of a kiss.

Everyone in the car howled and teased Kristina Rose.

"Oh, shut up. We're all adults here, and half of us are married or almost there anyway."

"Speaking of almost there," Summer said, at last feeling better about leaving Ben behind for the evening now. "Where are we going?"

"I told you, it's a surprise," Elise said at the exact same moment that Jennifer said, "To Austin."

"Well, there goes the surprise!" Elise groaned.

"Really, Elise. Get over it. I mean, where else were we going to go?" Kristina Rose asked. "Were we going to drive into the Gulf of Mexico?"

"Maybe, but now we'll never know," Elise

whined. "Fine, fine, just take the blindfold off. The whole surprise is spoiled now anyway."

Summer rubbed at her eyes after the heavy cloth was untied. "I really don't know why you had to kidnap me, or why we couldn't have just gone to the Rusty Nail."

"We do that every week," Elise said as she took one hand from the steering wheel and used it to fiddle with the buttons on the radio. "Tonight needs to be special. It's not every week one of our best friends marries one of our other best friends. Right, Kristina Rose?"

"Pressure much, Elise? Yeah, I'll probably marry Jeffrey one day, but he hasn't exactly asked yet. Besides, we have a lot to keep us busy with the restaurant. We're not in any hurry."

"Yeah, not like Miss Cinderella's Castle over here," Maisie teased Jennifer.

"What? It was perfect for us. I regret nothing."

"How about you, Summer?" Maisie asked. "Any regrets?"

"About marrying Ben? Not a single one," she said, feeling with every beat of her heart that this was the greatest truth she had ever known.

"Well, Maisie, I guess it's up to you and me to hold down the fort," Elise said with an exaggerated sigh.

"What fort?" Maisie laughed. "Fort spinster? Yeah, okay."

"Get with this century," Elise teased. "We're not spinsters. We're strong, independent women who don't need a man to define them."

"Excuse me!" Jennifer and Kristina Rose cried together.

Then an old song by Destiny's Child came on the radio, and they all belted out the lyrics at the top of their lungs as they drove deeper into the night.

Summer could barely see the road before them, but somehow she knew it would be okay—this bachelorette party, her life with Ben, all of it. That's what taking a leap of faith was all about. It meant continuing forward even if you didn't have all the steps figured out just yet.

First, she'd have whatever fun her friends had planned for tonight, and then she'd go back to the business of living out her forever with Ben at her side.

Ben watched as Summer's friends wrapped a blindfold around her head and stuffed his bride-to-be into the passenger's side of her own car. He would have laughed at the ridiculous, over-the-top antics of Summer's bridesmaids if he weren't so distracted by his rage.

"Ben," his mother said softly, coming up behind him. "Can we please go home now?"

"Sure, let's go." Ben and Susan started the walk toward home, seeing as they still couldn't afford a car with his low-paying job at the Market and Susan out of work for the past several years. They didn't make it too far past the edge of the parking lot when an old truck pulled up beside them. The window rolled down to reveal Pastor Bernie.

"Hop in," he said, and Ben knew the pastor wouldn't take no for an answer, no matter how much Ben needed the fresh night air to cool his head.

A few short minutes and they were home. Unfortunately, so was another former resident of 1701 May Lane.

"Should I stick around?" the pastor asked, looking from John Davis to Ben and back again, worry furrowing his auburn brow.

"I'm going inside," Susan announced, hopping out of the car and walking on unsteady feet toward the door.

"Please don't upset him," she said to her ex-husband, her voice drifting in through the truck's open windows as she reached around John to unlock the door, then disappeared inside.

"Thanks for the ride home," Ben told the pastor, and he took a deep breath before getting out of the truck and slamming the door behind him.

"I told you to stay away," he said through gritted teeth, trying his best not to look at the man he had once called "Father."

John strode confidently toward his son and placed a hand on Ben's shoulder, but Ben shook it off and gave the man the coldest look he could summon, once again wishing his eyes had the ability to produce actual daggers.

"Ben, I love you, and I want to be a part of your life."

"Now?" Ben spat. "Now! Where were you when Mom practically killed herself with drinking? Where were you when I was about to follow in Stephen's footsteps and shoot my brains out? Where were you when we couldn't afford to pay the mortgage? When anything important happened during these last few years? That's right. You were off with your younger, happier family, pretending we didn't exist."

"Son, it's not like that. I can explain—"

"Why bother? Actions have always spoken louder than words. Except there's one word that speaks volumes—*Stephanie*."

"Your little sister? She—"

"She's not my sister, and you're not my father.

How could you do this to Mom? How could you do that to Stephen's memory?"

The other man looked genuinely distraught, but Ben didn't care. Even if he regretted things now, this fresh remorse came much too late. "Please, let me talk," Ben's father begged. "I've never stopped—"

"Why should I let you talk? It's way too little way too late. You're not part of this family anymore, and that's a choice you made. Not Mom. Not me. *You*."

John drew closer to his son and opened his arms, whether to request a hug or give Ben an easy shot wasn't entirely clear.

Still, Ben mumbled, "If you try to touch me again, I'll punch you in the face."

Another car door slammed, and a second later Pastor Bernie was standing there beside them. He towered over both the Davis men by a good half foot, giving him an exaggerated sense of authority. "John, it's been a long time," he said. "Can I take you out for a drink? To catch up?"

Ben's father cast another doleful glance at his son before clapping Bernie on the back and turning back toward the driveway. "Yeah, that sounds good. As long as you let me treat."

"I wouldn't have it any other way," Bernie said with a chuckle, which cut through the tension at once.

Ben stood rooted in place until the illumination from the truck's headlights faded back to black night. *Mom*, he remembered in a panic and raced inside, hoping it wouldn't be too late.

He found his mother on the sofa. A single lamp lit the room as she stared down at a full bottle of vodka. She held the liquor firmly with both hands, staring at it so intently Ben wondered if she could even see it at all.

He racked his brain for the right words. Should he tell her he understood, remind her of how much she stood to lose, how far she'd come? Before he could settle on what to say, Susan spoke out in a strange, emotionless voice.

"We alcoholics are good at hiding. We hide our sickness, hide our problems, even hide our booze. Did you know I had this one stashed away in the attic just in case?"

She laughed, but it held no mirth, no anger, nothing.

"I still remember the day your father left. It was a Tuesday, like today. He took everything he could fit in the car and then just drove away. I didn't stop him. I wanted him to go. Somehow I had come to blame him for all our problems, even for what happened with Stephen. I looked at him, and I just felt so angry." Her entire posture stiffened as if also recalling a muscle memory from those rage-filled days.

"The hate had become so huge that there was no more space for love, for understanding, for anything else. Our marriage was dead long before your father left." She looked up at her son and studied him as if only just realizing he'd joined her. "He did the right thing, Ben. I'm every bit as much to blame as he is. Probably more so."

"Mom, no, that's not the way it was. He—"

"Is a flawed human being just like you, just like me, like Stephen. You can't hold on to your rage forever. Otherwise you'll never learn how to cope. You'll run straight to a Band-Aid solution. Maybe you'll become a drunk like me. Maybe your hate for your father will fill you up so full that you won't have any room left to love Summer."

Ben bristled. His voice came out harsher than he intended, but that was one accusation he could not allow to slip by. "I will *always* love Summer," he said through clenched teeth.

Susan sighed and set the bottle of vodka down on the coffee table. "And believe it or not, I will always love your father. It's not the same as it was, but we had many good years together. He gave me the best things in life. He gave me you, Ben."

"But he hurt us."

"I hurt us far more than he did. I hurt him, too. When I was drinking, I wasn't myself. It's like I surrendered myself completely to the drug, and the drug possessed me, became me. Your father had married the smart, funny, good singer, Susan. He hadn't married Booze-an." She laughed at her own joke, the light began to return to her eyes.

"Please forgive your father. Let go of the resentment, start your married life with a clear head and heart. And for the love of all that is holy, take this bottle away from me before I forget *my* head."

Ben grabbed the bottle from its spot on the coffee table and headed toward the kitchen to empty it down the drain, but his mother stopped him. He turned to face her, but she'd gone back to staring straight ahead. He fixed his eyes on her wavy brown hair as she spoke.

"Just because our marriage didn't last doesn't mean yours is doomed to fail. Learn from the mistakes your father and I made. You love learning, so learn this: People make mistakes, but they are not defined by them. Learn, grow, and never forget to put love first. Put God first, and you'll have many happy years together."

"Thanks, Mom." He wanted to hug her then, but he didn't want to upset her in her fragile state, and the full bottle of vodka burned in his hands. He needed to expel this poison from their lives.

"And please find a way to forgive your father," his mother said when he returned from emptying the bottle in the sink. "If not for him, do it for yourself. Ben, you deserve everything in life. And above all else, you deserve to be happy."

"So do you, Mom. So do you."

She let out a dry laugh. "I've been happy in my life. Now, more than anything, I want you to have everything you've always dreamed of for yourself and everything I've dreamed of for you as well."

"But what about you, Mom?"

"You being happy makes me happy. One day you'll understand. When you're a parent yourself."

Ben smiled to himself as he pictured a future version of Summer wearing the blue-patterned smock of St. Joseph's as she delivered their first child into the world. There was so much in life he had yet to experience, so much more he wanted.

But he couldn't understand why his mother had given up on those things for herself.

"Besides Summer, you're the only family I've got," he pointed out. "We need to take care of each other. I'm not giving up on you, Mom."

"Okay," she whispered. "Then don't give up on your father, either."

FIVE

The girls arrived in Austin roughly an hour later. Elise parallel parked in front of a bank downtown, and everyone clambered out of the car.

"It's so easy parking this tiny thing," mused Elise, who was more accustomed to driving a pickup truck. As soon as she'd closed the door behind her, she was off like a shot, leading them deeper into downtown Austin.

"Okay, so we're here. What's next?" Maisie asked, rubbing her hands together as the group followed Elise down the sidewalk. Summer would have likely asked Maisie to be her maid of honor if Elise hadn't claimed the role for herself. After all, it was Maisie who had first invited Summer into their circle. And while Summer admired Elise's take-charge attitude, she preferred Maisie's gentler approach to leadership. Then again, Elise's brashness was also what made them all love her so much, and it also made her the perfect pairing with the milder-mannered Kristina Rose.

Elise continued forward without answering the question. She turned right at the intersection, and they all waddled after her like baby ducklings. Summer was thankful she'd worn flats with her rehearsal dress instead of heels like she'd originally planned.

"Where are we going?" Jennifer asked, quickening her stride to match Elise's.

"Dunno," Elise answered, continuing forward with determination.

"Excuse me?" Kristina Rose chimed in, easily keeping pace with them now that she had lost nearly one hundred pounds. "What do you mean you don't know?"

"I *mean*," Elise said, drawing out that second syllable far too long. "That I don't know where we're going."

"How could you not know?" Summer demanded. "You're the one who planned this whole thing!"

Elise stopped suddenly and turned to face the others. They stood in a huddle blocking a large portion of the sidewalk. Luckily, downtown Austin wasn't too busy at nine o'clock on a Tuesday night. Still, the few would-be passersby, who had to step out into the street to navigate around them, did not seem happy about it.

Elise grabbed Summer's hand and clasped it in her own. "You have the whole rest of your life planned out, you know? Marriage, house, kids, PTA, all of it. So I thought it might be nice if we celebrate your last day as a single woman by not having a plan, by just going where the wind takes us and enjoying whatever happens next."

"It's not very windy," Maisie said.

"Not the point, Mays. *The point* is things are going to change from here on out, for Summer, for all of us. They've already changed heaps for Jennifer. Everyone's getting married. Next will be the babies, and soon karaoke night at the Rusty Nail will have to be put on permanent hold."

"I'm not married," Kristina Rose said with a sigh. "I'm not even engaged."

"But you will be," Elise said gently. "Then it will be Maisie, and where does that leave me? *Alone*, that's where."

"I had no idea you felt that way," Kristina Rose said. "You've been my best friend forever. Nothing would ever change that."

"I hope you're right, but plans change, intentions

fade away. That's why tonight I just want to live for the moment. It'll be good for *all* of us. Let's go wild. Let's get crazy. Let's just focus on having a good time together, the way we always have."

"So karaoke?" Jennifer giggled.

"Well, that's up to Summer," Elise said. "What'll it be?"

"Karaoke sounds perfect," Summer said, looping her arm through Elise's and pulling her into her side. "Looks like there's a bar up there. Let's go!"

They all linked arms and ran down the street, eliciting curious glances from a line of cars as they idled at a red light.

"A round of whatever you've got on tap! My friend's getting married, and we're here to celebrate!" Elise, whose cheeriness had thankfully returned, shouted toward the bartender as they entered and took their seats. That was Elise; she owned every room, even those she'd never stepped into before. Whether or not she believed it, she'd make the right man very happy one day. Summer just hoped he'd be as good at taking orders as all their friends were.

"You know I can't drink." Kristina Rose, who was normally all smiles, scowled. The upset expression didn't blend well with her dark features. "Not after my surgery."

"I'll happily drink yours once I finish mine," Elise said with a laugh.

"Excuse me," a pretty blonde woman around their age said as she squeezed in beside them in their booth. "Did you say you're getting married?" She looked at Maisie, who shook her head vehemently, sending her bobbed haircut swishing back and forth.

"Me? Heck no. These two are the wifeys. Well, she's a wifey, and she's an almost-wifey." She pointed to Jennifer, who waved and offered a smile, and then to Summer, who nodded. Something about this stranger seemed mighty familiar, but Summer just couldn't put her finger on it.

"Congratulations. You must be so excited!" their new friend said. "Do you mind if I treat you to this round?"

"If you want to buy us drinks, you can go right ahead, missy," Elise shouted over the music that played in the background.

"It's not *missy*," she said. "It's Jordan."

That's when Summer finally realized who this woman was. "Oh my gosh, you're Jordan Tate!"

The pop star beamed at them and raised her hand. "Guilty as charged."

"Do you know her from somewhere?" Kristina Rose asked.

"Yeah, the top-forty billboards. She's Jordan Tate.

She's like the next Taylor Swift! Haven't you heard that song 'You're My Kind of Guy'?"

"No way!" Jennifer and Maisie squealed together and then burst into the chorus of the song Summer had just referenced.

"You guys," Summer hissed. "Be cool!"

Jordan laughed. "It's okay! I always love meeting fans, but please don't let Tay hear you call me the next *anything*, especially not the next *her*. She hates it when people say that."

"Oh my gosh, oh my gosh," Jennifer sang. "She knows T-Swift, too!"

"Well, my break's up," Jordan said, rising back to her feet. "Thanks for coming out tonight. Enjoy the drinks, enjoy the show, and enjoy your wedding. Bye!"

The Sweet Grove girls stared slack-jawed after Jordan as she wove through the crowd, took up her mic, and sang her newest single, "Let's Make a Night."

"See," Elise said proudly. Summer could practically see her chest puff up with pride. "When you don't make a plan, anything can happen."

They clinked their glasses together, and for now—just for the night—Summer was all too happy not to have a plan.

* * *

Ben hated leaving his mother alone with all the heightened emotions swirling around from his father's return, but she insisted he head to Jeffrey's as planned for his bachelor party—if you could even really call it that.

"I've got Doritos, pizza rolls, and Mountain Dew. Good?" Jeffrey said, greeting him at the door.

Ben eyed the array Jeffrey had laid out before them. He'd taken extra care to plate up the snacks nicely. "That's *different*," Ben said with a shrug.

Jeffrey shrugged back. "I thought about cooking, but that seems to go against the spirit of what tonight is."

"Which is?"

"Just kicking back and bro-ing out, like we did in high school—eating junk food, laughing at stupid jokes, and playing video games until the sun comes up. You up for it?"

Ben sighed and sank onto the couch. "After the night I've had so far, that sounds perfect."

Jeffrey grabbed two controllers and booted up his Xbox. "Grab a controller and pick your kit."

Ben laughed. "It doesn't matter what I choose; all the middle schoolers out there are going to tear us apart online." It had been so long since he and Jeffrey had done this, he could scarcely remember how the controller worked. Good thing it was like riding a bike, a little pink one with streamers.

"Maybe so, but at least put up a fight!" Jeffrey stuck his tongue between his teeth as he expertly navigated the screen.

That was when the doorbell rang.

"Oh good, there's the stripper I ordered," Jeffrey said, popping to his feet.

Ben's face must have shown his horror. Summer would not like this—not one bit. Ben wasn't sure he'd care for it much, either. After all, Summer was the only girl for him, had always been the only girl for him.

"Relax, man," Jeffrey said with a laugh. "Remember that part about stupid jokes? It's just Beckett."

That sudden feeling of horror did not fade with this news. "Beckett? You invited Beckett?"

"Well, kind of. He actually invited himself. And after Liam cancelled on us, I just couldn't say no. I mean, we all used to be tight back in high school."

"Yeah," Ben grumbled. "But Beckett still acts like he's in high school even now."

"Which is perfect for tonight," Jeffrey pointed out. "He *is* the school gym teacher, and you and me need more friends anyway. The girls are all so tight, and we barely ever make time to hang out. We need more friends, Ben, and there's no time like the present. Besides, we could use a ringer that thinks like those kids online."

Ben decided not to mention how he'd been hoping to turn to Jeffrey for some advice about his upcoming marriage. Even though Jeffrey and Kristina Rose weren't engaged yet, Ben knew his friend was just biding his time, waiting to afford a truly lavish affair for his princess. Luckily for Ben and Summer, her aunt Iris had insisted on footing the full bill for theirs.

"Ben, how's it hanging?" Beckett returned with Jeffrey a moment later, clunking a giant box of Pabst Blue Ribbon on the coffee table.

"The usual," Ben mumbled.

Beckett sank down onto the couch beside him and mussed up Ben's hair in an overly familiar gesture that unsettled Ben. "I couldn't believe it when Jeffrey told me there wouldn't be any strippers at your bachelor party, so I figured we could at least make things interesting by turning this tired old video game into a drinking game."

"I don't really drink much," Ben said. Did Beckett not know his mother was an alcoholic? That alcohol had nearly ruined Ben's life many times over?

"Well, you do tonight!" Beckett crowed, tossing a

can of the cheap beer over to Jeffrey and then handing one to Ben.

Jeffrey shot him an apologetic glance before opening the beer and chugging.

"No, thank you." Ben put his unopened can on the coffee table and turned his attention back to the game screen.

Beckett shrugged. "More for us. Right, Jeff?"

Jeffrey grabbed another controller from the entertainment center and handed it to Beckett.

They sat in silence for a few short moments before Beckett decided that the silence needed to be filled. He'd always been like this, which is why Ben hadn't been too interested in spending any time with him after high school despite being neighbors.

"So little Ben's getting married?" Beckett said with a laugh. Ben gritted his teeth. Spending time with Beckett was only just barely better than having another confrontation with his dad. What had Jeffrey been thinking inviting him?

"I'm taller than you," Ben said, refusing to make eye contact with his uninvited guest.

"Yeah, but it took you long enough. Remember how shrimpy you were freshman year? I never would have thought you'd land a woman like Summer Smith, let me tell you. Never would have guessed such a fox could have sprung from the same gene pool as old Iris, either." He raised his beer and took a drink.

Ben didn't know what to say, and apparently Jeffrey didn't either.

"Let's just play the game," Ben said. He couldn't wait to open fire on Beckett's character or to make an excuse to bow out early and go home. Same team or not, Beckett just might wander into some friendly fire . . . or a grenade.

They played for about an hour, getting walloped by their online rivals every single time.

"Sorry," Jeffrey said when Beckett stumbled toward the bathroom several beers later. "I didn't realize he was still the exact same guy we knew in high school."

"Seriously, exactly the same. I hated him then, you know."

"Yeah, me too." Jeffrey gave a resigned laugh. "I think we just hung out with him because he got all the girls."

"Not anymore, though," Ben said, lightening up a bit.

"That's right. Now it's all us, little Ben." Jeffrey clinked his water glass to Ben's. He'd had one beer to appease Beckett, who hadn't noticed that he was the only one drinking.

"Don't let Summer hear you call me that. I'm

already not good enough for her."

"No, man, you're not. But I'm not good enough for Kristina Rose either. Still, whether or not we deserve them, they love us. For better or worse."

"Maybe. I just hope that doesn't change."

"Why would it change?" Jeffrey asked with a look of pity.

"Forget it. It's just pre-wedding jitters, I guess." Ben stuffed his worries about his father back down and returned his attention to the game.

He'd take it one game at a time, one day, one minute. It wouldn't be much longer until this was all over. This "party" would end, his father would go back home, and Summer would be his forever.

For better or worse.

Oh, how he hoped he could give her *better* every single day of the rest of their lives together.

SIX

Summer awoke with a dull pounding in her head, briefly forgetting where she was. She sat up with a start, surprised to see Elise in bed beside her.

"Good morning, Summer Sunshine!" her friend shouted, making the pounding that much worse. "I was beginning to think you'd never wake up."

"Is she awake?" Kristina Rose asked upon exiting the tiny hotel bathroom, her hair and makeup already perfectly in place.

"Kind of," Summer groaned as she rubbed the sleep from her eyes.

"Wow, what a night!" Jennifer squealed, plopping down onto the foot of the bed and bouncing happily on the springs.

"You can say that again!" Maisie added as she picked up the phone on the nightstand and signaled for everyone to be quiet. "Yes, I'd like to order room service," she murmured into the receiver.

Maisie nodded and then asked, "Well, what do you recommend?"

Twenty minutes later, they all sat cross-legged on the pair of queen beds with a huge assortment of eggs, bacon, ham, grits, and baked goods piled high on a bellhop cart parked in the narrow space between the beds.

"This doesn't seem very healthy." Kristina Rose frowned as she poked at a danish pastry.

"We've got ya covered, girl." With a flourish, Maisie removed a silver lid from a plate of poached eggs, melon, and turkey sausage.

"So . . ." Elise said between bites of her third strip of greasy bacon already. "Today you woke up to me, but in just four more days you'll be waking up beside a sexy piece of man meat."

"Elise!" Kristina Rose looked embarrassed enough for all of them.

"What? She will be, and soon enough so will you," Elise pointed out.

"Not really appropriate, though, especially considering you and Ben used to date," Maisie mumbled.

"Yeah, like a million years ago! I'm just trying to ask Summer if she's ready is all."

"It's okay," Summer said with a laugh, picking up the danish Kristina Rose had rejected and taking a huge, delicious bite. "I'm ready. And nervous. And excited. And a hundred other things."

"Well, of course you are!" Jennifer said as she swayed from side to side, her eyes huge and alert despite the early hour. "You get used to it really fast, though, and I mean that in the best possible way. I *love* being Mrs. James, and you'll *love* being Mrs. Davis."

"It must have been so weird for you," Maisie said, glancing toward Jennifer as they ate. "All at once you became a wife and a mom with almost no time to prepare for it."

"Hey, I had plenty of time, even though I know you're still mad about not being able to come to our wedding. It really was a spur-of-the-moment thing, I swear! Anyway, it's easy when you're in love, and I'm double in love with Liam and Molly Sue. But this is about Summer, not me. How are you doing with everything?" Jennifer reached out and gave Summer's shoulder a squeeze, leaving behind a bit of grease in the process. Oh, well, at least they were all still in pajamas.

Summer thought about this for a moment. How

was she supposed to feel on the eve of her wedding? She felt so many things, but more than anything, she felt just as she always had—like herself. "I'm ready," she said at last. "I've been ready for a long time."

Everyone nodded and continued to dig in to their breakfast array.

But Summer no longer felt hungry. She thought back to the rehearsal dinner the night before, the absolute rage her fiancé displayed when his father turned up with hardly a moment's notice.

Kristina Rose noticed right away. "What's wrong, honey?" she asked, placing her plate to the side and coming to sit directly beside Summer.

"I'm still worried about Ben."

"You think he may have cold feet?" Elise asked. "I can tell you for a fact that boy has never been happier in his entire life. What's there to worry about?"

"He was really upset when his father showed up at the diner," Kristina Rose mentioned. "But Jeffrey promised to take good care of him."

Summer sighed. "Maybe, but the only example he has of a marriage ended horribly, and I know how his brain works. He must be tearing himself apart right now."

"Your parents' marriage wasn't so great, either, right? And you don't think you're doomed to repeat their mistakes, do you?"

"But Ben and I think differently. I guess it's the whole glass half-full, glass half-empty thing. Because of his depression, his glass is always running on empty."

"But if you put your half glasses together, then you have a full drink," Jennifer said, jumping to her feet and coming to stand in front of them. "That's what marriage is."

"A shared glass?" Elise asked with a hearty laugh, still seated the same as before. "I like it."

"Are you upset that your parents aren't coming?" Kristina Rose asked once everyone had stopped laughing.

"Let's get one thing straight here. I only have *one* parent. I never knew my dad, and my stepfather is the furthest thing from a parent out there. But yes, I'm sad my mom couldn't make it out."

"What's her excuse?" Elise asked with a mouth full of even more bacon.

"Elise, seriously!" Kristina Rose shouted.

"What? If I had a daughter, I wouldn't miss her wedding for the world."

"It's okay," Summer murmured. "My mom lets me down a lot. I'm used to it. Besides, I have Aunt Iris."

"And don't forget your cousin, Sunny Sunshine!" Jennifer said, eliciting a fresh round of laughter.

"And you have Susan," Maisie added. "She's a mom to you now, too."

"Do you think we should have invited her to come to Austin with us?" Kristina Rose asked with a frown.

"Nah, not her scene," Summer said. "And we'll have plenty of time for just us before the wedding. And remember, we'll be living together after, too."

"You are a saint," Elise said. "I love Mrs. D and everything, but man."

"It's not like that," Summer answered. "I love her and want to make sure she stays on the path to recovery. The worst thing Ben or I could do would be to leave her on her own. She's had enough heartbreak already without losing Ben, too."

"Like I said, a saint." Elise winked as she reached for the last piece of bacon.

"So everything's falling into place," Maisie said, seeming just as relieved as Summer was beginning to feel.

"Just about."

"Uh-oh. What's left?" Kristina Rose asked gently.

"Well, besides the problems with Aunt Iris's garden and Ben's dad, my wedding dress still isn't ready yet. It was supposed to be ready almost a month ago, but the boutique I ordered it from keeps telling me they need more time."

"But the wedding is Saturday!" Jennifer reminded them all.

"I know, I know. That's what I get for ordering something custom rather than just finding something nice at David's Bridal or something. But I plan on getting married once and *only* once. I just want it to be perfect, you know?"

"Well, of course you do!" Kristina Rose said, shaking her head. "Shame on them for keeping you waiting right to the final hour."

"Where's this shop? I think maybe I should pay them a visit to, uh, express the urgency of the situation," Elise offered.

"Normally, I'd say no to Elise's thuggish ways, but you're kind of out of options here," Maisie said.

"It's here in Austin," Summer said as she pictured Elise putting the fear of God into the slacking designer. Elise could be pretty scary when she wanted to be, but the specialty wedding shop had their fair share of bridezillas, too. Would Elise be able to get the job done? Well, she at least had a greater chance of succeeding than Summer did by herself.

"Perfect. We'll swing by on the way out, and God willing, leave with your wedding dress."

God willing, indeed.

* * *

Ben had hoped to have a heart-to-heart with his best man during their gaming bachelor party, but Beckett had ruined that possibility entirely. Now he felt more lost than ever, as worries gathered in his mind like storm clouds.

Would he be a good husband, or was their marriage doomed to fail just as his parents' had? He was his father's son, for better or worse—usually worse.

Normally he'd throw himself into work as a distraction, but Maisie had given him the full week off with pay, insisting he be available for whatever last-minute wedding details popped up.

So given his huge stretch of free time and his agreement with Summer to spend these last few days as singletons apart, he went to the only place he could think to go, the place that had been his safe harbor before Summer took over that role for him. He went to the library.

He could use this time to study up on the various marriage guides housed in the self-help section at the back of the library. He could learn how to be a good husband, put his mind at ease.

If he came equipped with all the solutions, then whatever problems might one day arise wouldn't seem quite so daunting. At least that's what he tried to convince himself.

Still, there was something about the feel of a book in his hands that put him at ease—if only for the moment. He gathered a few books from self help and a few more from the social sciences section then headed over to his favorite table to tuck in.

"Hi, Ben," the librarian, Sally, said, striding over and taking a seat across from him. She smiled, showing off the gap between her two front teeth. Her pale skin seemed to glow underneath the fluorescent overhead lighting.

"Hi, Sally," he said, offering her a quick smile. Sally, at least, was one thing that never changed. She was always here at the library, excited to hear about his latest research.

"What are you doing here? I thought you'd be busy with Summer all week, not sitting here, reading . . ." She craned her neck to read the heading at the top of Ben's book. "Reading up on marriage traditions of the Indian subcontinent."

"They walk around a fire seven times for luck," Ben said, setting the book aside. "And Summer said we should spend a few days apart before the wedding."

Sally frowned, her dark hair swinging gently as

she shook her head from side to side. "Trouble in paradise?"

"No, Summer is perfect. It's just . . ." He grimaced. It was strange talking about these things with Sally. They'd only ever discussed books and knowledge, not relationships. "It's just," he finished, "that I'm *not*."

Sally nodded, but kept her expression otherwise blank. "Me neither, as a matter of fact. Few of us are." She snorted and picked up the book.

"Summer is," he said, getting straight to the heart of the problem as he stared down at the words on the page until they blurred. Summer was so far above him, he didn't have a prayer's chance of rising to meet her—and the last thing he wanted to do was to bring her down. He'd always known this, of course, but with their wedding so close, it weighed all the heavier on his shoulders.

"Yes, I know," Sally said, and for a moment she sounded angry. But when Ben glanced over to her, she wore the same smile she always had.

"Ben," she started, wetting her lips and taking a deep breath. "There's something I need to—"

They both startled at the sound of loud footsteps echoing across the otherwise quiet library.

"Your mother told me I might find you here,"

John Davis said, barging over toward their table, completely out of place in his surroundings.

Sally cleared her throat and pulled away quickly, returning to her desk upfront.

Both men watched her leave. When John turned back toward his son with an expectant look in his eyes, Ben said, "Yes, I'm here. Now please go away." He couldn't even bring himself to look at his father as he stomped over to Sally's desk.

"What were you going to say?" he asked her, trying to pretend they were still alone in the sanctuary of the books.

She shook her head, her eyes wide as she looked from Ben to his father and back again. "It's not important. I'll leave you two to talk." She rummaged through a stack of papers on her desk, trying to appear busy.

"I came all this way to see you," John said. "Please can't you give me five minutes?"

"I could have," Ben shot back. "I could have given you those minutes one of the many times I was cleaning up after Mom because no one else was around to do it, or you could have taken your five minutes when I was having a conversation with myself as to whether I'd rather hang to death or take a quick bullet. Your time is up."

"Ben, I'm sorry I wasn't there then, but I'm here now."

"That's not going to be good enough," Ben said, taking a moment to stare into his father's hollow eyes before storming out of the library and heading anywhere but here.

Not good enough seemed to be the theme of the week. Oh, how he prayed it wouldn't become the theme for the rest of his life.

SEVEN

Summer was starting to wish she hadn't asked Ben for some time apart before their wedding. Sure, planning and dealing with last-minute disasters kept her busy most of the time, but whenever she had a spare moment to stop and think, her thoughts found Ben.

Now she was lying in bed, reading through old comment threads and articles on a popular wedding website as a last-ditch effort to see if she'd missed anything important for her own.

But really all she wanted was for Ben to be her husband and for this ridiculous time apart to end. Was it a bad sign she could hardly make it a few days on her own?

A soft knock sounded on her door, then her aunt pushed her way into the room.

"C'mon," Aunt Iris said. "Let's go get gussied up for the big day."

"We're not doing hair and makeup until the morning of. You know that." Summer returned to her iPad, but Aunt Iris didn't leave.

She stomped over, grabbed Summer's hand, and inspected it closely. "Ink stains," she said before raising her own hand demonstratively. "And my old wrinkled hands are always caked in dirt."

"So a mani-pedi then?" Summer placed the tablet on her nightstand and rose to her feet. There was no denying Aunt Iris when she had an idea. Besides, the bit of pampering would be nice.

Aunt Iris laughed. "If that's what they're calling it these days, then sure. I just think we need our nails done. I'll even drop Sunny Sunshine off at the groomer to get his nails trimmed and beak shined for the big day. What do you say?"

"I say you have yourself a deal," Summer answered as she searched her closet for something to wear to the salon. A thought struck her. "Can we invite Susan, too?" she asked.

"Best get used to calling her *Mom* soon," Iris said with a wink.

"Is that what people do? It just feels so weird. *Mom* is my mom. Well, sort of."

"My sister is a lot of things, but we both know she hasn't been mother of the year here."

She hated thinking of her mother. The woman practically felt like a stranger and had ever since she'd remarried. Her aunt, on the other hand, had always been far more attentive to Summer's needs even though they only saw each other a few times per year while she was growing up. Summer frowned, but immediately rearranged her features into a smile. "That's why I'm lucky to have you, Aunt Iris."

"The feeling is mutual, kiddo. Now let's vamoose."

Summer called Susan's house phone as Iris drove them both toward the house Summer would soon call home, too. Ben's mom, of course, jumped at the invitation and soon all three women were seated with their feet in mini baths of sudsy water as a single salon worker flitted back and forth between the three of them, smiling sweetly as she worked but not saying much to anyone.

"It's been so long since I've had any pampering," Susan said after a long, relaxed sigh.

"That's just not right," Iris said, clucking her tongue.

"Do you not like getting manicures . . . *Mom*?"

Summer asked, trying the strange word out and receiving a smile from Susan when she did.

"Oh, honey, you don't have to call me that if you don't want to. It's so weird. I never quite got used to it with John's parents." She sighed again—something she did often these days. "Now it doesn't matter much, I guess."

Summer reached over and squeezed her soon-to-be mother-in-law's hand. "I want to. I just have to get used to it first."

"And you need to get used to spoiling yourself, dearie," Aunt Iris said from her seat on the opposite side of Summer.

Susan leaned her head back and looked toward the ceiling as she spoke. "I just haven't seen the need without a fella in my life. You know how it is."

"Nonsense," Iris exclaimed. "I've never had one, at least not for long, and I do just fine. You get dolled up for yourself, love. Not for a man."

"She's right," Summer added. "Even though that's exactly what I'm doing right now. Getting pretty for Ben on our wedding day."

"We'll let this one pass," Aunt Iris said with a knowing smile.

"Susan, let's make a monthly date of this, shall we?" Iris leaned so far forward in her chair as she strained to see Susan that Summer prepared to catch her in case she toppled over. "Lord knows we both need a little extra TLC, and we're family ourselves, now that our kids are getting married."

Susan forced a smile and sighed again. "I can't exactly afford a luxury like this."

"Don't say no," Summer said gently. "She's absolutely right. Plus we're adding another salary to the household, and you deserve it. We can all use a little more Aunt Iris in our lives."

"I'm going to miss you, Sunny Summer."

"But I'll just be a few blocks away. You know that."

"Nope, Susan and Ben are stealing you right out from under my nose."

Susan started, "Iris, I didn't know you felt that way. I—"

"She's only teasing. Don't worry about it." Summer shot her aunt a warning look. It would definitely be good for Susan to spend more time with lighthearted Iris, but the much more serious woman needed time to get used to Iris's teasing ways. As of now, she took everything at face value and was still learning how to relax and to get through her day without turning to alcohol whenever anything upset her. "She's like my weird aunt and overprotective mother all rolled into one."

"I guess I can go back to just being weird Aunt

Iris now that you have a new mom here." She leaned back in her chair and let out a happy sigh—a stark contrast to the dramatic sighing Susan was always doing.

Susan worried her lip. "What happened to your mother, Summer? Why isn't she coming? I'm sorry to pry, but you just don't talk about her, and it doesn't seem to bother you much that she's not here."

"Of course, it bothers me." Summer sighed, too. Between the three of them, they had probably let out enough air to fuel a hot-air balloon. "But I kind of gave up on my mom a long time ago. We all have our own choices to make. I don't like the ones she's made, but I can't change them for her. Maybe one day we'll reconnect, but until then, I have plenty of family right here."

"Hear, hear!" Iris said, raising her bottle of water in salute.

"Well, I'm proud to call you my daughter," Susan said with a shy smile.

"Me, too!" Iris added.

They both reached out to squeeze Summer's hands at the same time, and she knew then just how lucky she was to call Sweet Grove home and to have these women as family.

* * *

Ben trod up the steps of the little white church on First Street. So much had changed since he had come here as a child, holding tightly to his mom's hand on one side and his big brother's on the other, being promised an ice cream if he was good during the service. The church hadn't split off into a separate Sunday school class until Ben had long stopped attending and would have been too old for it anyway.

For years, the church had been a symbol of the many things wrong in Ben's life—the God who had turned a blind eye to Stephen's suffering, the topic of many of the fights between his parents, the gathering place of a community that Ben had never quite felt a part of.

How much things had changed.

Now the First Street Church was the only place Ben could think to go for answers and clarity—yes, even more so than his beloved library. God had become one of the only constants in his life. God and Summer . . . except Ben didn't feel worthy of Summer, yet he knew he could come to the Lord flawed and broken.

Which is what he did now, walking reverently toward the altar. The large stained-glass window cast dancing swatches of colors from above, creating an ethereal feel. Fresh carpet that didn't quite match the original ran down the aisle, and lingering sawdust lined the edges of the sanctuary.

Termites, Ben remembered. *They'd tried to tear the church down, but luckily it had been built on rock instead of sand*, he thought, remembering the parable his mother had taught him in childhood.

He reached the front pew and sat with his elbows on his knees, his hands in his hair, his head bowed. In the nearly one year since his return to the church, Ben had asked God for many things: patience, understanding, a solution to his mother's problems, a happy future for him and Summer.

Today he had so many questions swirling about his head that he wasn't even sure what he *could* ask of God. He pictured Summer's smiling face promising to love him forever and always, then his mother's face clenched with anguish. He saw Jeffrey so worried about being nice that he forgot to look out for his own interests. He saw his father's new wife, Megan, unaware of their pasts.

And he saw his father, standing beside him, begging for a fresh chance. His features looked so much like Stephen's, which only made it more painful to look upon the man whom he blamed for so many of his life's worries.

What did it all mean? How did Ben fit into this patchwork community?

He tried to call up Summer's image again but remained stuck on his father, whose likeness had now merged with Stephen's in his mind.

Anger, so much anger. And regret.

A part of him knew he needed to let go, to forgive, give his father another chance. But what if, in allowing his father back into his life, he only ended up hurting worse? What if Summer or his mother took the brunt of that pain?

Would that make him like Jeffrey, who still struggled with expressing his own needs and desires?

It was all so confusing.

"Please grant me clarity," he murmured. "Amen."

When he looked up, he saw Pastor Bernie sitting on the pew across the aisle with his Bible in hand. "Clarity," he echoed. "A good prayer."

"I didn't see you here when I came in."

"That's because I've only just arrived. Tell me, Ben, is there something weighing on your heart? Something you'd like to discuss?"

"I don't know."

"All change is stressful, you know. Not just the bad things, but the good, too. Weddings tend to cast a harsh light on our lives, our ambitions. They put everything into perspective." Pastor Bernie smiled, keeping his gaze fixed straight ahead at the stained-glass window before them.

"That's definitely true." Ben sighed and steepled his fingers. "Will all of this go away once the wedding is over?"

"No," the pastor said with a smile. "But it will go away once you surrender it to God."

"Believe me, I'm trying." As Ben said this, the pastor turned toward him and offered a thoughtful glance.

"It's hard with your father here, remembering everything that happened with your family."

"I wish he wasn't here. It's so much easier to pretend he doesn't exist, that he died with Stephen." Ben felt guilty for even thinking the words, let along saying them aloud. But if he couldn't be honest with the pastor and with God, he could never hope to be truly honest with himself or with Summer, either.

"Fathers," Bernie said with a deep exhale. "Mine beat me six ways to Sunday. Until Sundays were the only thing I lived for, finding comfort from my heavenly Father, getting away from the one on earth for a couple short hours each week."

This was news to Ben. The pastor spent so much time listening to others' problems, he almost never mentioned his own. Ben felt selfish in that moment, knowing his father had never raised a hand to him, yet somehow Pastor Bernie could forgive and Ben could not. Now it was Ben who looked away as he spoke. "I had no idea," he mumbled. "I'm so sorry."

"The Lord doesn't send us anything we can't handle. I had a hard time growing up, but the situation also gave me a solid base of faith, and *that* I have never regretted. We need trials in order to grow, to discover who we really are."

"That's what I worry about," Ben admitted. "Finding out who I really am in the end. *He's my father.* What if it's only a matter of time before I follow in his footsteps? Before I let Summer down?"

"We are each our own person, and we are each a child of God. You make your own choices, Ben. Make them to the glory of God, and you will always do well." The pastor laughed and pulled up his shirt sleeve to show off a dark-blue band around his wrist.

"Remember these from, oh, twenty years ago? WWJD: What Would Jesus Do? Sure, a lot of folks wore them as fashion statements, but to me it means so much more. That's why I wear it to this day, to have that reminder right on my body, sitting above a vein that leads straight to my heart, a heart for God."

"Awesome," Ben said, unable to think of any other response.

Bernie chuckled. "It is pretty awesome, isn't it?"

"I still don't know what to do," Ben admitted.

"Give it to God," Bernie answered. "The fact that

you want to do right by those in your life speaks volumes. Remain faithful, continue coming to God, and remember to ask yourself, 'What would Jesus do?'"

"That's it?" Ben asked. "Usually you have much more specific advice."

"That's it. It's the advice that encompasses all advice."

Just then a perky series of chimes and whirls sounded from Pastor Bernie's pocket. "Excuse me," he said, standing to fish his cell phone from the front pocket of his khakis.

He smiled at Ben and nodded as he listened to the speaker on the other end of the line. Ben could hear a frantic female voice, but not the words she was saying. The room grew quiet, and the pastor's smile faded into a deep frown. The lines on his forehead furrowed with worry.

He simply said, "Okay, I'm on my way," and then placed his phone carefully back into his pocket.

"Is everything okay?" Ben asked, not wanting to pry but figuring it would be ruder still to ignore the newly arrived elephant in the room.

"I'm not sure, but just like you, I'm going to give it to God." Pastor Bernie approached Ben and reached out his hand to clasp Ben's in a firm shake, a promise. "I need to leave town for a couple of days, but I promise I'll be back in time for the wedding. I wouldn't miss it for the world."

Ben hugged him goodbye and watched as the pastor rushed away. He said one more prayer for whoever it was who'd called Pastor Bernie in such a frantic state and then lifted himself to his feet and headed home.

EIGHT

Summer had always been the type of girl who liked to try a bit of everything. That's why she had changed her major so many times in college. It's why it had taken her an embarrassingly long time to realize Sweet Grove was meant to be her home and Ben to be her husband—and it was why she'd decided to hire Mabel's, Ernie's, and Fred's to cater the wedding.

She loved all three restaurants, and even more so loved their proprietors. How could she let any of them down? So it was decided; her wedding would serve German fare, pizza, and down-home cooking in a quirky amalgamation that represented their little Texas town perfectly.

Today everyone had gathered at Mabel's to coordinate and make final arrangements for the big day, which was the day after tomorrow. There was a bit of a battle as to which restaurant would host, but ultimately Mabel's won out because it had the largest walk-in cooler, which was needed to store the abundance of food and confections.

As for the wedding cake, they had three of those, too—a black forest cake from Ernie, tiramisu from Fred, and strawberry shortcake from Kristina Rose, Jeffrey, and Mabel.

"Don't you think it might be a bit much?" Maisie asked as she and Summer unloaded the truck she'd brought over from Sweet Grove Market.

"It's *much* too much," Summer answered with a laugh. "But that's kind of why I love it!"

"Still I can't believe you didn't ask the market deli to cater, too." Maisie stopped laughing and fixed Summer with a stern look. "Way to leave us out of the party."

"Oh no!" Summer cried, practically dropping the flat of fresh strawberries she was carrying. "I didn't realize!"

Her friend laughed and jabbed Summer with her elbow. "I kid, I kid. There's no way I want to be a part of the battle raging in there." She pushed open the door with her hip, and they were immediately greeted with the sound of bickering.

"*I'm* doing the rolls," Fred of Fred's Pizza Company insisted.

"And *we're* doing the biscuits," Mabel shot back, standing on the tips of her toes so she could look her nemesis in the eye.

"What about rye bread?" Ernie asked in his unique accent, German mixed with a heaping dose of Texas flavor.

Both Fred and Mabel whipped around to stare at Ernie, who raised his hands and backed away slowly. That was when they spotted Summer standing awkwardly near the door.

"Tell the man we don't need rolls *and* biscuits," Mabel demanded, charging toward her.

"And tell *the woman* she has a huge menu and could offer something else instead," Fred spat back.

"It's not my fault you have such a limited range!" Mabel shouted.

"That's it!" Kristina Rose motioned toward Jeffrey, and they both came over to stand in the newly formed circle by the door. "You are retired, Mabel. Do you know what that means?"

"My name, *my* diner," Mabel said with a pout, but already she had deflated a bit. "And you know I'm only semiretired."

"M," Jeffrey said calmly, despite the tension that filled the air all around them. "You know you can't handle this stress. You trusted Kristina Rose and me to run things here. We promise that the diner will be well represented at the reception."

Kristina Rose nodded adamantly. "That's right, and Jeffrey is even making a surprise dish to be unveiled for the first time at the wedding."

Mabel softened, but only just. "What about the biscuits?"

"Let Fred do the bread. I've got much bigger things planned." Jeffrey's eyes sparkled with the promise of something special, and Summer saw that one day he would be a spectacular father. For now, though, he and Kristina Rose had their hands full with their sixty-something pseudo-kid.

"Fine, fine." Mabel held her hands up in surrender, and Fred bowed toward Jeffrey.

"Thank you, sir," he said. Then he said to Summer, "I promise it will be the best bread you've ever tasted." He gave one last look to Mabel before walking triumphantly toward the kitchen.

"Is it safe now?" Ernie asked, returning to the dining room once Fred had departed.

"It seems as long as the three of you aren't all in the same space at the same time, then we're golden," Maisie mused. "It's almost as if we need a referee!"

"Well, why didn't you say so earlier?" Elise rummaged in her purse until she found a metal whistle, then strode over to the small congregation near the door. She always had one on her as part of her coaching duties for the girls' softball team. She'd recently taken on volleyball as well.

"Perfect," Summer said with a laugh. "Elise, you're in charge."

"Oh, you're going to regret that!" Maisie said with a massive eye roll.

Elise blew her whistle and pointed toward Maisie. "Ten points from Gryffindor."

"Really!" Jennifer shouted from across the room. "You should have seen that coming, Summer."

The door swung open, and everyone turned, expecting to see Susan and Iris returning from their errand to pick up more supplies from the craft store. Instead, Ben's new stepmother, Megan Davis, poked her head inside, almost as if she were afraid to bring in the rest of her body.

"I hope it's not an imposition," she projected in her strong newscaster voice. "There's just so little to do at the bed and breakfast, and I thought maybe I could be of use here. If it's not okay, I can—"

Summer gave her a smile. Perhaps she and Megan could work together to repair some of the damage between Ben and his father. This was decidedly a good thing. After all, there was no reason she and

Megan couldn't be friends, especially considering how close they were in age.

"Hey, relax. Come inside. Weddings are about bringing people together, right?"

A huge smile spread from cheek to pretty cheek as Megan reached down to hold the hand of her toddling child and guide her inside.

"It's Stephanie, right?" Jennifer asked, rushing over to pick up the little girl. "I recently became a mom, too. Isn't it the best thing in the whole wide world?"

"I always thought I was a career girl, but then Stephanie came along, and now I dread going to work most days. I'd stay with her all day if we could afford to. Are you and Ben hoping to start a family soon, Summer?" Megan asked kindly as she drew a series of toys and board books from her diaper bag and set them out for the little one.

It was a good question, and one none of her friends had really asked yet. They were too busy teasing her about the wedding to have switched over to pressing her about a possible pregnancy. She supposed that would happen the moment they were back from the honeymoon.

"Yeah, I want to be an aunt!" Elise said, spinning her whistle on her fingertip.

Or right now. Now that Elise had hold of it, she wasn't going to let it go.

"I didn't mean to start anything," Megan said apologetically. "I just need time to prepare if I'm going to be a grandma at thirty." She giggled and kissed little Stephanie's head.

"Yikes, and I thought it was weird I have a seven-year-old at twenty-five," Jennifer said with a giggle.

"She's her stepdaughter," Maisie explained.

"But it doesn't feel that way one bit," Jennifer added. "It's like Molly Sue has always been mine. Well, you know how it is. Right, Megan?"

"Definitely," the young wife answered. "Don't worry; you don't have to call me Mom," she said with a laugh.

Summer smiled and nodded. Okay, so this was more than a bit odd.

"I know it's weird," Megan answered as if reading Summer's thoughts. "I never thought I'd end up with an older man, and I'm not a gold digger," she added with a pointed look.

"Then what drew you to Mr. Davis?" Elise blurted out what was on all their minds.

"I know things are hard with him and Ben, but John is a good man. He's been through a lot and wants to be better because of it. I just wish Ben would give him a chance." She looked expectantly toward Summer.

"I may be able to help with that," Summer said with a whisper. "But you have to promise me you'll do exactly as I say. I don't want Ben to get hurt."

"Oh, sweetie. Neither do I. I only want both our guys to be happy."

Summer smiled and got back to work. That was all she wanted, too.

Ben found himself once again sitting among the worn books of the Sweet Grove Public Library. With Jeffrey at work, Summer and Susan tending to the wedding plans, and his father lurking in some unknown place in town, he really had nowhere else to go. He figured his father wouldn't think to look for him here again, since he'd already ambushed him once at the library. Lightning wasn't supposed to strike twice, after all . . . or so they said.

Today, he hoped the words surrounding him would give him the inspiration to pen his own. He still hadn't managed to write vows that accurately captured everything his heart held for Summer. He'd wanted them to be perfect, but at this point, he'd be more than happy to settle for *good enough*.

A realization that left him feeling incredibly guilty.

This writer's block thing he'd heard so much about seemed very real now that it'd trapped him in its evil clutches. He felt as if he were stuck in a giant block of ice, able to see what he wanted but unable to budge even a fraction of an inch to get it.

Block, indeed.

He groaned as he tore another page from his notebook and crumpled it into a ball.

"Uh-oh. This doesn't look too good," Sally said, striding over and taking a seat beside him.

"This writing stuff is hard. I don't know how you and Summer do it," he mumbled.

"What are you writing? Or what are you *trying* to write?" She smiled knowingly and reached for the wad of paper he'd just chucked onto the floor.

"Roses are red, your eyes are blue . . ." she read aloud. "*Oh, I see.* Having trouble with your vows?" She raised an eyebrow and waited.

"I don't know why it's so difficult. I know what I'm feeling. I just have no idea how to say it."

Sally cleared her throat and dropped her gaze to her fingernails, which were freshly painted with dark-purple polish. "It *should* be easy if you're passionate about the words . . . Are you?"

He stiffened in his chair. "I love Summer more

than anything, but I'm not a writer. What would you say if you were me?"

Sally looked up at him then, an unfamiliar lightness in her features as she spoke. "I'd say that you've loved her since the moment you first saw her, that life is more of everything with her in it, happier, sadder, sweeter, just all-around better. I'd say that you can't possibly picture a future without her at your side and that every time you think about the shared life that lies ahead, you want to pinch yourself because surely something this wonderful has to be a dream."

"That's perfect. Keep going!" Ben turned his notebook to a clean sheet and began to scrawl Sally's beautiful words in ink.

"Love," Sally continued, her smile spreading wider, "is never a mistake. It's patient and kind like the Bible says, but it's also destined. I believe you only get one chance at a perfect love, and that everything else is but a sliver in comparison. Everyone has that one perfect person their heart beats for, even if they don't know it yet."

Ben continued to write down Sally's beautiful words, only looking up at her once he'd finished recording them all. "Is there anything else?" he asked.

She nodded and whispered, "I love you."

Ben laughed in response. "Well, of course, I'm

going to tell her I love her in my vows. Those were the only good words I managed to write myself."

Sally shook her head, and her long hair cascaded over her shoulders and brushed the surface of the table. "No. I love you."

This was weird. Sally never talked about feelings, nor did they spend time together outside the four walls of the library. She'd always been a bit unusual, socially awkward like Ben had been before Summer changed him for the better. Was she just trying to express how much his friendship meant to her? Was she playing a joke on him? Testing his loyalty to Summer? He honestly didn't know what to think.

He laughed again, but Sally's expression remained serious. He cleared his throat and said, "I love you, too. You have been such a good friend all these years."

"No, Ben, that's not what I mean." She grabbed his fingers and squeezed them in her cold hands. "I love you, and we should be together."

"Sally, I . . ." His mouth remained open, but no more words came out. Why weren't the words coming out?

"It's okay," Sally whispered, leaning in closer until her face was mere inches from Ben's. "I know you love me, too. You always have."

How could this be happening? He'd always cared for Sally, sure, but he'd never thought of her as anything more than a friend and fellow bookworm. He racked his brain, thinking back over all the moments they'd shared together, trying to find the precise moment in time when he'd given her the wrong idea, but every attempt came up blank.

Sally licked her lower lip, drawing his eyes down, and the next thing he knew she was kissing him. Her kiss was tight but urgent. It took rather than gave. It was all wrong.

He contemplated this, still trying to make sense of what was happening. When he realized his thoughts were preventing him from acting, Ben shot to his feet so quickly his chair fell back onto the carpeted floor.

Sally stared up at him, her eyes large and intelligent like a cartoon owl. Her normally pasty skin was lit with a warm pink glow. The usual hesitation in her demeanor had all but disappeared as she rose slowly with an awkward smile on her face as she approached Ben once again.

"No!" he shouted, even though they were in a library, even though the few other patrons were all watching them intently.

"Ben, give me a chance to explain myself," she insisted.

"What's there to explain?" He cursed under his

breath and crossed his arms over his chest. "I love *Summer*. I'm marrying *Summer*. This is very wrong."

"It's not too late to call it off. Run away with me, Ben, far from Sweet Grove, far from everyone. We can make our own life, a happy life. We could be so perfect, Ben."

"Are you listening to me? I love Summer. I want to marry Summer. I'm sorry, Sally, but I don't feel the same way you do. I've never thought of you as anything more than a friend, and honestly now I'm going to have a hard time even considering you that. Where did this all come from? And how could you possibly think this was okay? I…I…" He ran his hands through his hair, a sharp headache forming behind his temples.

Was nothing sacred? Were no places safe anymore?

He stumbled out of the library, Sally on his heels.

"Where are you going?" she called after him.

"I don't know," he mumbled back, even though she'd lost the right to know.

"Can we please talk about this?" she begged.

"I'm done talking," he said before breaking into a sprint. The one person he longed to speak with more than anything was off limits until their big day. Would she still want to marry him when she found out what Sally had done? What he'd somehow invited, somehow let happen?

Now, more than ever, he knew in his heart he would never be good enough for Summer Smith. He also understood how easy it was to make mistakes—especially in the heat of the moment when emotions were running high. Sally had certainly acted out of character tonight, and she could never take back what she'd done. The only thing that could be changed was Ben's attitude toward what had happened. He didn't think he could—or should—ever forgive Sally, but what about his father?

His heart softened as he recalled how hard life had been for all of them in the wake of Stephen's death, as his mother fell deeper and deeper into her addiction. She'd said that she had driven his father away. Could that be true?

And he'd returned now, said he wanted to make things right between them.

Could Ben forgive the past?

He'd have plenty of time to figure that out. Right now he needed to focus on his future with Summer. Tomorrow was their wedding day, and he needed to do everything in his power to make sure it was the best day of their lives.

NINE

Summer woke up on the morning of her wedding, hardly able to believe that the big event had finally arrived. Before the day was through, she'd be Mrs. Ben Davis, something she never would have guessed when she first arrived in town nearly one year ago.

Yesterday Aunt Iris had made a point of banishing Summer from the last-minute preparations. "Rest up, buttercup!" she'd said with a wink before heading off to oversee the various activities herself.

Oh, it had been difficult to wait at home with nothing to do!

She'd been so close to calling Ben but ultimately decided against it. Just one more day and they'd be together forever, she'd reasoned.

And today was that day—the day slated to be the best of her entire life.

She took her time in the shower, soaking in the hot water and singing merrily to herself. When she returned to her room to throw on an outfit for the hairstylist's, she saw that she had several missed calls.

Uh-oh.

Taking a deep breath, she called Elise first.

"Finally!" her friend shouted on the phone. "I've been trying to get ahold of you all morning."

Summer decided not to explain that she'd only been away for about twenty minutes as she listened patiently to Elise's harangue.

"I didn't want you to worry, *but*." Elise paused.

A tiny kernel of dread formed in Summer's stomach. "Wait, worry about what? What's going on?"

"The bridal shop. They were supposed to have your dress ready to go yesterday, but when I went, they said something about finishing touches and perfect fit and all that. So they told me to come back today. I thought, okay, they are cutting it really close here, but if they insist. So I—"

"Elise, please! Cut to the chase. What's the problem? Is my dress not ready?"

"No, it's ready. I have it with me right here." Elise hesitated.

"Then?"

"I have the dress, but, umm, not my truck. It was stolen, I guess."

Pop, pop, pop went the dread. Summer couldn't help but shout into the phone, "You guess? How did that happen?"

"Well, I got to the shop this morning at the time they told me, but they still weren't ready and asked me to wait while they added beads or lace or something. I honestly don't know. Anyway, an hour later, finally I have the dress, but my truck isn't where I left it. I've been up and down Austin, well as far up and down as I could get on foot while carrying a giant garment bag. It's just gone. I'm waiting for the police, so I can file a report. But . . . yeah."

Summer pressed the bridge of her nose and did her best to keep her voice calm even though inside her mind was reeling. "Elise, the wedding is in two hours. Not only do you have my dress, but you're my maid of honor!"

"I know, I know. I'll call around and get somebody to come get me, but I'm not sure we'll make it in time. Not unless we go really, really fast—like double the speed limit fast. Do you want us to?"

Before hanging up, Summer made Elise promise not to risk losing life or license by driving too fast. Now, she had two huge problems to solve. First, she'd need to figure out what to wear, and then she'd need to find a new maid of honor. Unfortunately, she didn't have time to solve either, because the very second she hung up with Elise, Jennifer called and announced, "Summer, we've got a problem."

"I know!" Summer whined when really she wanted to scream. "I can't believe Elise is going to miss the wedding!"

"Wait," Jennifer squeaked. "Elise is going to miss the wedding? How is that possible?"

"That's not the problem? Oh no. No, no, no. What *other* problem do we have?"

Jennifer's voice was meek as she explained, "Molly Sue is throwing up everywhere. We thought she might be coming down with something, and, boy, did she ever. She's got a fever, too. I just don't think it would be a good idea to have her go ahead as the flower girl. She'll get all your guests sick and probably cover them in puke, too."

"Oh," Summer said with a frown. She couldn't be mad at a child for falling ill, but her wedding party was dropping like flies here.

"I'm so sorry, sweetie," Jennifer said. "I'll still come, but Liam is going to have to stay home with Molly Sue."

"It's okay," Summer said. "I hope she feels better soon."

"Do you think maybe Jeffrey's dog, Toto, could be the flower girl?"

Summer laughed at the thought, making her feel slightly better despite the tremendous stack of stress that was stacking up on her like bricks ready to bury her alive. "This is my wedding, not a circus," she said at last. "And we already have a *parrot* ring bearer. Besides, you know how much Toto drools on everything."

"Okay, then I'll do it," Jennifer offered apparently without a second thought.

"*You'll* be flower girl?"

"Yeah, I even have experience. I was a flower girl for the Browns when I was seven."

"Wasn't that, like, eighteen years ago? Aren't you a little old to be flower girl now?"

"Hey, desperate times, desperate measures. It's not my fault you rejected Toto for the role."

Summer promised to think about it, then hung up with Jennifer and scrolled through her missed calls, surprised to see one from Ben. She pressed the button to call him back, and Susan answered, short of breath.

"There's a terrible storm!"

Summer peeked out her window and only saw sunshine.

"Not here," Susan continued, as if reading her

thoughts. "In Chicago. That's where Pastor Bernie is. He was supposed to fly in early this morning, but his plane is grounded because of the storms."

"Are you telling me that my pastor is going to miss the wedding?"

"Afraid so, but Elise is ordained, right? Can she stand in?"

"Elise is stuck in Austin."

"What?"

"No time to explain. I've got a lot of work to do."

"I'll see you at the church, okay?"

Susan coughed. "Uhh."

"*Oh no*, what's wrong with the church?" Summer couldn't believe this. Alanis Morissette's wedding day rain had nothing on Summer's parading circus of catastrophes here.

"It's the termites," Susan said, pausing to take a long, loud gulp of something Summer desperately hoped was water. "There's been a resurgence, and the new floor isn't holding up like it should."

"So can't we just walk around the hole or whatever?"

Another cough. "Again, I'm afraid not."

"What are we supposed to do then?" Summer moaned.

"Well, the original plan was to get married in your aunt's garden. Can you still do that?"

"I'll ask her, I guess."

"Summer, are you okay?"

"I'll be fine. Just a lot to do first."

"I hear you on that one. The good news is it will all be over in a few hours."

As they said goodbye, Summer wondered how she'd gone from excitedly awaiting her wedding to just wanting it to be done. Was this normal? Was this her fault for being too laid-back about the planning? If she'd been more of a bridezilla, maybe all this wouldn't be happening now.

She didn't know the answers to her problems or even why they were piling on all of a sudden, but she needed to start by making a decision.

Her dream wedding dress was holed up in an Austin police station, which meant she needed something to wear.

Ben hadn't been able to sleep that night. Too much weighed on his mind, and he'd never quite learned how to shut off his brain on command. He was already awake when his mother barged into his room that morning.

"Ben, we have a problem," she said, sinking onto the mattress beside him.

He sat up and rubbed what little sleep he'd had from his eyes. "I know." He couldn't help but sigh. "Sally kissed me."

Susan let out a low whistle and shook her head. "Well, that's a new one for me."

"Just forget it for now. Is Summer okay?"

"Oh, yeah. She's fine. The wedding, on the other hand . . ."

This was it. Ben had always known he wasn't good enough for Summer, and now she'd finally realized it, too. She'd probably rushed off to her hometown in California, never to look back on Sweet Grove—or Ben—again.

"I can see those wheels turning," his mother said. "Cut that out already. Like I said, Summer is fine, but there's a problem with the church and the dress and Elise and Molly Sue and Pastor Bernie."

Ben listened in horror as Susan outlined the many problems that had sprung up that day. "Is that all?" he asked when she stopped to take a long, drawn out breath.

"For now," she said with a laugh.

Ben hadn't thought his brain had room for any more panicked thoughts. He was wrong. He eyed his mother with disbelief and said, "Why are you laughing? This isn't funny at all!"

"It's just . . . sometimes you have to laugh to keep

from crying—or drinking, you know," she offered with a shrug.

His mother was right, of course. She'd come such a long way in the past year. After years of surrendering to the bottle, she'd finally gotten the help she needed. She didn't wake up one day and find the addiction was gone. No, it had been a lot of hard work, but work that was well worth doing.

It made him think of his love for Summer. He wasn't good enough for her yet—not in his estimation—but each day he could put in the work. He could spend the rest of his life loving her the best he could, trying as hard as he could to be worthy of her.

If his mom could do it, then so could he. He could defeat his own demons, the ones that liked to whisper in his ear and cause him to doubt everything. He'd spent too much time already questioning God, Summer, his father, himself.

It was time to just live.

"Mom, hang on a sec." Feeling energized now, Ben rummaged through the kitchen drawers until he found a steno notepad. He wrote down all the issues his mother had just reported. "Is that everything?" he asked, holding up the paper so she could see his list.

When she nodded, he jotted a number next to each issue. "So our biggest problem is the lack of a pastor."

She nodded again.

"Who else do we know who's ordained?" He tore off a fresh piece of paper and handed it to his mother along with a pen. "Make a list and then make some calls."

"Okay, I've got this. But what about the other seven hundred problems?"

"I've got them, starting with finding a place to actually get married."

Susan raised an eyebrow at him and crossed her arms. "You really figured out all the answers within the span of two minutes?"

"No time to explain. Just find us an ordained minister, and I'll call you when I have some more solutions. Can you coordinate with Summer's aunt Iris to keep them in the loop, too?"

"I feel like a fancy 1950s' secretary," Susan quipped. "I'm on it, boss."

As his mother headed off to place her series of calls, Ben thought through all the various places in town that were big enough to hold a wedding. They had at least one hundred guests, which meant few places were big enough to accommodate everyone. They'd had it right the first time in selecting Iris's large backyard garden. The weather was nice, which meant the outdoors was still a viable option.

Ben thought of all the places that were important

to him and Summer. Many of his favorite memories with her had taken place around the old orchard—the bridge where he'd proposed, the well where they'd made their wishes together, the trails they loved to jog down side by side.

Suddenly, he knew exactly what to do about this snare, too. Amazing how well he could work things out when he focused on solving real issues instead of just rehashing imagined ones over and over again.

But he would need help to implement his plans.

As it was, the entire remaining bridal party was already buzzing around trying to fix all the sudden problems. Ben didn't have time to call a long list of people to see who was available. He needed to get someone his first try, and unfortunately he had a pretty good idea of who would be ready and willing to help.

He swallowed his anxiety and dialed the number to the bed and breakfast where his father and Megan were staying for the week.

"Dad?" he asked.

"Ben! I'm so glad you called." He could almost hear the relief in his father's voice.

"Can you meet me at the church? I need your help."

"See you in five minutes."

True to his word, Ben's father was already waiting

on the steps of the little white church when Ben arrived himself. John Davis rushed over to hug his son, and this time Ben let it happen. Sure, his father had let him down many times before, but he was here now at the time it mattered most, when Ben had no one else he could turn to.

And that counted for something.

It counted for a lot.

Ben explained the problems and his plan, then asked, "Do you think you and Megan can help with that?"

"Yes, of course. We'd be happy to, but before you go, can I please tell you what I've been trying to say all week?"

Ben sat down to brace himself, and John sank down beside him.

"I know I did a lot wrong after Stephen."

Ben took a deep breath and failed to hold back the tears that had already begun to form.

John reached over and clapped his hand on Ben's back. "I messed up. I know it, and I'm sorry."

Father and son looked at each other for a moment, then Ben allowed the tiniest smile to slip onto his face. It was a smile of forgiveness, of something new.

His father smiled back. He, too, had tears in his eyes. "I will always regret not trying harder to help your mother and you in the aftermath of Stephen's death. The thing is that I was just as broken as you, and seeing your suffering, seeing Stephen's empty spot at the table every night when we sat down for dinner, well, it was just a constant reminder of how I'd failed you all.

"I convinced myself you'd be better off without me, so I left. I spent over a year punishing myself, Ben. But then by chance I met Megan, and she helped me to heal in a way I wasn't able to help you. In the same way it seems Summer has saved you from yourself, Megan saved me.

"She helped me get right with myself and, more importantly, with God. And all that left fixing things with you and your mother—that's why I'm here. I can't change the past. I can't change what happened with Stephen, as much as I wish I could. His life was way too short, and it's not fair. None of what happened was fair.

"But it's why, when my little girl was born, I couldn't think to name her for anyone other than Stephen. So that her life could be an homage to his, so she could live the years he wasn't able to, so that I would always be reminded of what I'd lost so that I could remember to cherish what I still had.

"I want to be there you for, Ben. I want the

chance to make things right. I want a relationship with you if it's not too late."

Ben folded his hands and propped an elbow on each of his knees as he thought. He already knew exactly what he wanted to say. It's what had kept him up all night. Now hearing his father voice the same things that were in his heart made it possible to say it.

He looked at the ground as he spoke. He couldn't afford to be distracted. He wanted to get these words exactly right, because they were the words that would start his new relationship with his father. Like the vows he would speak to Summer later that day, these words were a promise.

"We both lost ourselves to the past. There was so much pain weighing on our shoulders, we couldn't lift our heads to see into the future. But then God brought Summer to me and Megan to you, and they lifted us up with His help. I'm a better man because I love, and because I allow Summer to love me. It's like I spent all these years punishing myself for things that weren't my fault but felt like they were. And I blamed you, too. And God.

"I haven't regretted letting God back into my life. In fact, I've gained a lot from being able to come to Him with my problems.

"You and I, we lived through the same pain. We live with it now. We can be there for each other, understand each other in a way that no one else can. But if I continue to keep you out of my life, then neither of us can ever fully heal. I think we need to forgive each other to forgive ourselves. I didn't realize that until now, hearing how Stephen's death affected you the same way it affected me. I didn't know that.

"I always thought you and Stephen were the ones who had so much in common. But it seems I'm my father's son, after all. And maybe that isn't such a bad thing. *Dad*."

"We're going to be okay," John said, and Ben couldn't tell whether it was meant to be a question, a statement, or both.

He nodded. "We're going to be okay."

"Good. Now let's get to work on making this wedding the best day of your life."

Father and son shared a quick hug and then went their separate ways.

TEN

Summer walked up the hill toward the old wishing well she and Ben had visited together so many times before. She wore the same sundress she'd had on the first time she and Ben had met by accident at the flower shop.

As for the flowers, Aunt Iris had cleared out her entire shop and given each of their guests a potted arrangement to carry up the hill and line their makeshift aisle. Farther on, the apple trees bloomed with beautiful white and pink flowers, creating the most gorgeous backdrop imaginable.

Ben stood at the top of the hill with Jennifer at his side.

Her friend waved playfully, then cleared her throat and took on a more serious expression.

Jeffrey and Ben's dad stood with them, too. Ben's mom had happily replaced Elise as matron of honor, tearing up when Summer had asked her to serve the important role. Kristina Rose and Maisie also stood on the tiny hill, making their wedding party slightly lopsided, but Summer didn't care.

Other than the fact that Elise and Pastor Bernie were missing, everything was perfect.

When Summer reached the top of the hill, Aunt Iris gave her a quick kiss on the cheek and gave her hand to Ben's.

Ben wore a dark-blue tux with a clutch of daisies in place of a boutonnière. His eyes shone, reflecting her image back at her, showing she truly did live within his heart. "I love you," he whispered, surprising her as he leaned in to offer a kiss of his own.

"Hey, you've gotta wait until I give the okay!" Jennifer protested with a smile. She gave Ben a stern look and then broke into giggles. The happy-go-lucky Sunday school teacher wasn't exactly an expected choice, but she had been ordained once upon a time and loved them both dearly, which meant it made perfect sense for her to reside in Pastor Bernie's absence.

Ben shrugged and then said, "Oh, crap! I almost forgot!" He held up a finger so that Jennifer would wait as he reached into his pants pocket and took out his phone. Placing it on speaker, he pressed the call button and in an instant they were joined by Pastor Bernie.

"Would you, man?" he asked, tossing the phone to his best man, Jeffrey, and officially rounding out his side of the wedding party.

"Anything else we're forgetting?" Jennifer asked with one eyebrow raised toward Ben.

"Not a thing. Let's get this show on the road. I don't want to wait another second to marry this beautiful woman," he said, kissing Summer again though the timing was still all wrong. Summer didn't mind one bit.

"Okay, no more of that now. At least let me read my lines first, yeah?" Jennifer and Summer exchanged a quick glance and laughed. Most of the attending crowd joined in as well.

Above the giggles, a shout zoomed through the open air.

"I'm here! I'm here!" Elise ran wildly through the orchard wearing her signature jeans and a tank top. Her hair was a mess, and she panted so hard Summer had to wonder if she'd run here all the way from Austin.

Her friend came up and gave Summer a high five,

then sank to the grass in the front row to watch the festivities.

Jennifer laughed, cleared her throat, and began, "Dearly beloved . . ."

There were no more distractions as they reverently listened to Jennifer's scripture readings and prayers. No more laughter—but plenty of smiles—as Susan sang "Amazing Grace" in her beautiful soprano. Summer couldn't take her eyes off her handsome fiancé. Any minute now, Jennifer would say the magic words, and he'd become her husband.

"I understand the couple has prepared their own vows," she said, motioning to Summer and Ben and taking a small step back.

Ben gave Summer's hands a little squeeze. She expected him to reach into his pocket and take out a carefully folded paper filled with facts and cited sources, but he kept firm hold of her hands as he spoke.

"For weeks, I've struggled to find the perfect words to tell you on this day. But then I realized there are no perfect words, are no perfect people. Each of us is just doing the best that we can. I still don't know what I did to deserve you, Summer Smith, but rather than continue to question it, I'm going to focus on doing my best to make you happy every single day of the rest of our lives. I'm going to make sure you know how much I love you, how thankful I am that God has brought us together.

"As a student of history, I spend a lot of my time learning about the past. They say if we don't learn from our past, we're doomed to repeat it. But I also think if we don't look forward to our futures, we're doomed to let them pass us by. I don't want to miss a single second with you, Summer. Not a single one.

"I love you more than I ever thought it was possible for one person to love another, especially for me. But you took my broken heart, and you made it whole again with your love, your laughter, you.

"There are no perfect people, but, Summer, we are perfect for each other. For better or worse, richer or poorer, and all that other stuff, too, I look forward to all of it, knowing we'll face it together.

"I love you, and I can't wait to pave our future together."

"Ladies and gentlemen of Sweet Grove, I now present to you, for the first time ever, Mr. and Mrs. Davis!"

Ben grabbed his bride in his arms and swung her in for a dramatic kiss, the first kiss of the rest of their lives. And in that moment, everything melted away—

the people, the flowers, all of it—leaving just the two of them connected in that perfect moment in time.

When finally they came up for air, everyone clapped and cheered. Even Pastor Bernie whooped and hollered from the other end of the phone line. Yes, everyone had come out to be there. They were a town united in love. Ben had never felt so much a part of this town. But now he realized he'd always been one of them, and it was by his own doing he ever was an outsider.

Only Megan and little Stephanie missed the ceremony. They had agreed to stand vigil at the church and redirect the guests to the orchard, so that no one would miss out despite the last-minute change.

His father had volunteered to do it himself, but Ben had insisted he stand beside him at the altar, and Megan had happily stepped up to save the day. Now his new stepmother and little sister ran across the blooming field to join the rest of the wedding party. Ben looked forward to getting to know them both once he'd returned from his honeymoon with Summer—because *nothing* could keep him from that.

Rather than make a dramatic exit, Ben and Summer remained by the well for their receiving line. As the guests made their way up to offer their congratulations, Aunt Iris handed each one a coin.

Some were copper, some nickel, but all glinted beautifully in the sunlight.

"I'm so happy for you two," Elise said, hugging them both so tightly they could hardly breathe. "And so happy I didn't miss it after all." She held up her coin, a quarter. "Iris said that each of us should make a wish in honor of the new Mr. and Mrs. Davis. My wish is that each of you become more of who you're meant to be and that together you're able to realize the best versions of yourselves. I love you both and am so happy for you," she said as she tossed the coin down the stone well.

One by one, their friends and family made their way up, offering hugs, congratulations, and wishes.

Jennifer, Maisie, and Kristina Rose came together, hugging Summer between them. "Congratulations, Mrs. Davis!" they all cheered.

Ben beamed proudly. He would never get tired of hearing that.

"You're next," Summer said to Kristina Rose with a wink.

"Yeah, you all keep saying that." Kristina Rose rolled her eyes, but she obviously enjoyed the attention.

"We're all going to make our wish together to give it extra power," Maisie said, and the three friends approached the well together.

"We wish for babies!" they said, throwing their coins down in a fit of giggles.

Summer gasped. "Let us enjoy being married for at least an hour first!"

Ben pulled her in for a kiss. He couldn't wait to be a father, but he would let Summer decide when the time was right.

As the friends descended the hill, Sheriff Grant came toward them, dressed in his cleanly pressed uniform, though he had removed his hat for the occasion. "Ben and Summer, congratulations. I hope to one day find love like the two of you have, and even though I'm getting on in years, I still believe I will. Though I've got to say, I am so happy things worked out the way they did. Just think, if I'd had the courage to sign that card, then you'd never have thought the flower delivery was a mistake." He gave Ben a respectful nod, closed his eyes, and made his wish in private before letting go of the coin and retreating back down the hill.

"What did the sheriff just confess to, Ben?" Summer whispered for the brief moment they were alone.

"I think he just admitted that he has a secret crush on my mom."

"And what are we going to do about it?"

There was no time to discuss further, because

their next guest had already joined them on the hill. *Sally.*

She had huge tears in her gray eyes. "I'm so, so sorry," she said, hugging neither Ben nor Summer. "I don't expect you to ever forgive me, but I wanted to offer my congratulations and wish for your happiness." She threw the coin in the well and quickly descended back down the hill.

Summer looked to Ben with confusion marring her beautiful features.

"Sheriff Grant wasn't the only one with a secret crush," he confessed. "Sally tried to convince me to run away with her. She even tried to kiss me."

He'd expected Summer to look horrified, but instead she just shrugged. "That doesn't come as much of a surprise."

"What? I had no idea she felt that way. How could you have known?"

"She made it obvious from day one, but I knew if you wanted to be with her, you would have been already. I feel bad for her, though."

"What she did was totally wrong. How could you possibly feel bad for her?"

His beautiful new wife smiled sweetly at him, taking both of his hands in hers as if getting ready to say her vows all over again. "Ben, not everyone is as lucky as we are. Some people have to hurt for a much longer time before they can finally be healed by love."

"Then let's make a wish for them," Ben said, and Summer nodded.

They joined hands and approached the well that had served as their marriage altar. Already so many people had sent up wishes and prayers for their happy married life, so it only felt right to offer their wishes to those who hadn't yet been blessed the way Ben and Summer had.

So together they tossed a pair of coins down into the depths of the well, wishing with their whole hearts that love would make its way back to Sweet Grove to bless their friends.

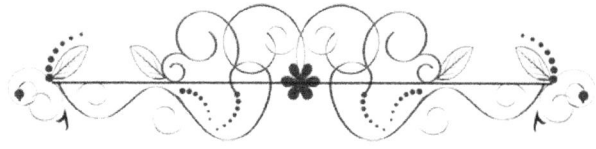

AFTERWORD

In 2012, I thought my life was falling apart. I had never expected to get divorced, but there I was, bitter, angry, hating myself, and completely spoiled on the idea of love. My eight-year relationship had taken a turn for the worse about a year and a half before then. I had opened a successful business, followed my dreams to write my first novel, and become a stronger, truer version of myself.

My ex, he didn't like that so much. I will spare you all the details, but just understand I found myself completely wrung out, broken, and frail.

I was at my worst, my weakest, when my true love finally found me.

Enter Mr. Storm.

He, too, was at his worst, his weakest. He was

actually contemplating suicide. It was bad. But we found each other. I wanted to date and have some fun, so I joined Match, Zoosk, eHarmony, all that stuff. And there I found Falcon, a writer like me, cuddling a gorgeous husky dog in his profile pic.

And so I reached out . . . as friends. I wanted a writing partner, not a life one.

But then the strangest thing happened. We met, and even though I still had relegated him to the friend box, I knew instantly that I wanted him in my life forever. Feelings like that don't just happen every day!

We became friends, good friends, best friends, and then less than a month later, one glorious Labor Day weekend, we shared our first kiss. And on December 1 that same year (yes, less than three months later!), we got married under the gazebo in a tiny park by our house. There were no bells, no whistles, no pomp or circumstance. Just love.

Four years later, here we are celebrating our anniversary. Still in love, still facing battles in our lives, but also fighting together. I don't know where I would be today, don't know *who* I would be, if not for Mr. Storm. He doesn't just make me a better person. He makes me myself, the person I actually am inside.

Do you know how freeing that is? I hope and I pray that even if you haven't found it yet, you will one day soon. Never settle for someone who suppresses your shine, who looks down on your accomplishments or mocks your interests. Don't let anyone tell you that you are not good enough. Hold out for *your* Mr. Storm, *your* happily ever after. Because, honey, he is out there, and once you find him, everything gets brighter.

All my love,
Melissa S.

MORE FROM MELISSA STORM

Sign up for even more free stories and uplifting messages from Melissa at www.MelStorm.com/gift.

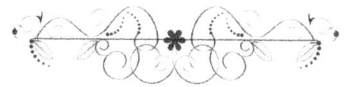

The First Street Church Romances

Love's Prayer

Love's Promise

Love's Prophet

Love's Vow

Love's Trial

Love's Treasure

Love's Testament

Love's Redemption

Love's Resurrection

Love's Revelation

* * *

The Sled Dog Series

Let There Be Love

Let There Be Light

Let There Be Life

* * *

The Cupid's Bow Series

When I Fall in Love

My Heart Belongs Only to You

I'll Never Stop Loving You

You Make Me Feel So Young

Total Eclipse of the Heart

Tainted Love

Eternal Flame

Take My Breath Away

I Want to Dance with Somebody

Somebody Like You

You Belong with Me

She Will Be Loved

What Makes You Beautiful

All I Want for Christmas is You

* * *

Stand-Alone Novels and Novellas

Angels in Our Lives

Diving for Pearls

A Texas Kind of Love

A Cowboy Kind of Love

A Wedding Miracle

Finding Mr. Happily Ever After

A Colorful Life

My Love Will Find You

The Legend of My Love

Splinters of Her Heart

* * *

Melissa also writes children's books and nonfiction as Emlyn Chand. Learn more about those works at www.EmlynChand.com.

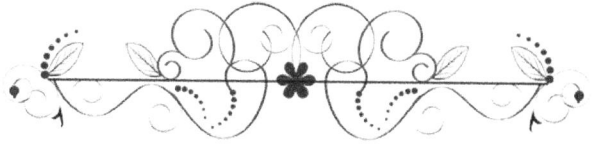

MORE FROM FIRST STREET CHURCH

READERS, FIND MORE BOOKS

Welcome to the tiny town of Sweet Grove, TX, where neighbors still care deeply about each other and the little white chapel on First Street is the heart and soul of all who live here.

It's a simple life–a good life–yet many here are suffering invisible pains. From alcoholism to divorce, hoarding, and even suicide, the struggles are real but so is the God who loves this town and all its residents. Through the darkest of times and the deepest of tragedies, each day provides a new chance to find faith, hope… and even love.

Our tiny town has grown by leaps and bounds,

thanks to the introduction of a new Kindle World. Many top Christian and Sweet Romance authors have already contributed their own stories to First Street Church, and many more are coming soon!

Come see what's available at
www.sweetgrovebooks.com.

* * *

AUTHORS, CONTRIBUTE YOUR STORY

Whose life will you change for the better? Will you bring new purpose to a troubled youth, redemption to a scorned elder, or perhaps salvation to the newest resident in town? Their fates and futures now rest in your capable hands.

www.sweetgrovebooks.com/authors

* * *

EVERYONE, JOIN OUR COMMUNITY

Welcome to Sweet Grove, TX. We're so glad you came for a visit! Please don't be a stranger. Come join our wonderful community of Christian Romance readers on Facebook. Make sure to sign up for the Sweet Grove Sentinel to stay up-to-date with all the latest and greatest First Street Church news!

www.sweetgrovebooks.com/community

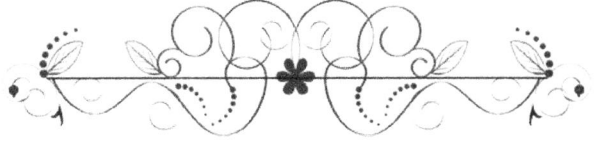

ABOUT THE AUTHOR

Melissa Storm is a mother first, and everything else second. She used to write under a pseudonym, but finally had the confidence to come out as herself to the world. Her fiction is highly personal and often based on true stories. Writing is Melissa's way of showing her daughter just how beautiful life can be, when you pay attention to the everyday wonders that surround us.

Melissa loves books so much, she married fellow author Falcon Storm. Between the two of them, there are always plenty of imaginative, awe-inspiring stories to share. Melissa and Falcon also run a number of book-related businesses together, including LitRing, Novel Publicity, Your Author Engine, the Author Site, and the Alliterates. When she's not reading, writing, or child-rearing, Melissa spends time relaxing at home in the company of her five dogs, cockatiel, and a rescue cat named Schrödinger. She never misses an episode of *The Bachelor*, because priorities.

www.MelStorm.com
author@melstorm.com

Made in the USA
Monee, IL
28 January 2021